THE LAST APPRENTICE

REVENGE Of THE WITCH

·BOOK ONE·

THE LAST APPRENTICE

REVENGE OF THE WITCH

Illustrations by
PATRICK ARRASMITH

JOSEPH DELANEY

SCHOLASTIC INC.
New York Toronto London Auckland Sydney
Mexico City New Delhi Hong Kong Buenos Aires

First published in 2004 in Great Britain by The Bodley Head, an imprint of Random House Children's Books, under the title *The Spook's Apprentice*.

ISBN-13: 978-0-439-90367-7
ISBN-10: 0-439-90367-X

12 11 10 9 8 7 6 5 4 3 2   6 7 8 9 10 11/0

Printed in the U.S.A.   23

First Scholastic printing, October 2006

The text of this book is set in Cochin.
Book design by Chad W. Beckerman.

FOR MARIE

REVENGE *of* THE WITCH

CHAPTER I
A SEVENTH SON

WHEN the Spook arrived, the light was already beginning to fail. It had been a long, hard day, and I was ready for my supper.

"You're sure he's a seventh son?" he asked. He was looking down at me and shaking his head doubtfully.

Dad nodded.

"And you were a seventh son, too?"

· I ·

Dad nodded again and started stamping his feet impatiently, splattering my breeches with droplets of brown mud and manure. The rain was dripping from the peak of his cap. It had been raining for most of the month. There were new leaves on the trees, but the spring weather was a long time coming.

My dad was a farmer and his father had been a farmer, too, and the first rule of farming is to keep the farm together. You can't just divide it up among your children; it would get smaller and smaller with each generation until there was nothing left. So a father leaves his farm to his eldest son. Then he finds jobs for the rest. If possible, he tries to find each a trade.

He needs lots of favors for that. The local blacksmith is one option, especially if the farm is big and he's given the blacksmith plenty of work. Then it's odds on that the blacksmith will offer an apprenticeship, but that's still only one son sorted out.

I was his seventh, and by the time it came to me all the favors had been used up. Dad was so desperate that he was trying to get the Spook to take me on as his apprentice. Or at least that's what I thought at the time. I should have guessed that Mam was behind it.

She was behind a lot of things. Long before I was born, it was her money that had bought our farm. How else could a seventh son have afforded it? And Mam wasn't County. She came from a land far across the sea. Most people couldn't tell, but sometimes, if you listened very carefully, there was a slight difference in the way she pronounced certain words.

Still, don't imagine that I was being sold into slavery or something. I was bored with farming anyway, and what they called the town was hardly more than a village in the back of beyond. It was certainly no place that I wanted to spend the rest of my life. So in one way I quite liked the idea of being a spook; it was much more interesting than milking cows and spreading manure.

It made me nervous though, because it was a scary job. I was going to learn how to protect farms and villages from things that go bump in the night. Dealing with ghouls, boggarts, and all manner of wicked beasties would be all in a day's work. That's what the Spook did, and I was going to be his apprentice.

"How old is he?" asked the Spook.

"He'll be thirteen come August."

"Bit small for his age. Can he read and write?"

"Aye," Dad answered. "He can do both, and he also knows Greek. His mam taught him, and he could speak it almost before he could walk."

The Spook nodded and looked back across the muddy path beyond the gate toward the farmhouse, as if he were listening for something. Then he shrugged. "It's a hard enough life for a man, never mind a boy," he said. "Think he's up to it?"

"He's strong and he'll be as big as me when he's full grown," my dad said, straightening his back and drawing himself up to his full height. That done, the top of his head was just about level with the Spook's chin.

Suddenly the Spook smiled. It was the very last thing I'd expected. His face was big and looked as if it had been chiseled from stone. Until then I'd thought him a bit fierce. His long black cloak and hood made him look like a priest, but when he looked at you directly, his grim expression made him appear more like a hangman weighing you up for the rope.

The hair sticking out from under the front of his hood matched his beard, which was gray, but his eyebrows were black and very bushy. There was quite a bit of black hair sprouting out of his nostrils, too, and his eyes were green, the same color as my own.

Then I noticed something else about him. He was carrying a long staff. Of course, I'd seen that as soon as he came within sight, but what I hadn't realized until that moment was that he was carrying it in his left hand.

Did that mean that he was left-handed like me?

It was something that had caused me no end of trouble at the village school. They'd even called in the local priest to look at me, and he'd kept shaking his head and telling me I'd have to fight it before it was too late. I didn't know what he meant. None of my brothers were left-handed and neither was my dad. My mam was cack-handed, though, and it never seemed to bother her much, so when the teacher threatened to beat it out of me and tied the pen to my right hand, she took me away from the school and from that day on taught me at home.

"How much to take him on?" my dad asked, interrupting my thoughts. Now we were getting down to the real business.

"Two guineas for a month's trial. If he's up to it, I'll be back again in the autumn and you'll owe me another ten. If not, you can have him back and it'll be just another guinea for my trouble."

Dad nodded again and the deal was done. We went into the barn and the guineas were paid, but they didn't shake hands. Nobody wanted to touch a spook. My dad was a brave man just to stand within six feet of one.

"I've some business close by," said the Spook, "but I'll be back for the lad at first light. Make sure he's ready. I don't like to be kept waiting."

When he'd gone, Dad tapped me on the shoulder.

"It's a new life for you now, son," he told me. "Go and get yourself cleaned up. You're finished with farming."

When I walked into the kitchen, my brother Jack had his arm around his wife, Ellie, and she was smiling up at him.

I like Ellie a lot. She's warm and friendly in a way that makes you feel that she really cares about you. Mam says that marrying Ellie was good for Jack because she helped to make him less agitated.

Jack is the eldest and biggest of us all and, as Dad sometimes jokes, the best looking of an ugly bunch. He is big and strong, all right, but despite his blue eyes and healthy red cheeks, his black bushy eyebrows almost meet in the middle, so I've never agreed with that. One thing I've never argued with is that he managed to attract a kind and pretty wife. Ellie has hair the color of best-quality straw three days after a good harvest and skin that really glows in candlelight.

"I'm leaving tomorrow morning," I blurted out. "The Spook's coming for me at first light."

Ellie's face lit up. "You mean he's agreed to take you on?"

I nodded. "He's given me a month's trial."

"Oh, well done, Tom. I'm really pleased for you," she said.

"I don't believe it!" scoffed Jack. "You, apprentice to a spook! How can you do a job like that when you still can't sleep without a candle?"

I laughed at his joke, but he had a point. I sometimes saw things in the dark, and a candle was the best way to keep them away so that I could get some sleep.

Jack came toward me, and with a roar got me in a headlock and began dragging me round the kitchen table. It was his idea of a joke. I put up just enough resistance to humor him, and after a few seconds he let go of me and patted me on the back.

"Well done, Tom," he said. "You'll make a fortune doing that job. There's just one problem, though. . . ."

"What's that?" I asked.

"You'll need every penny you earn. Know why?"

I shrugged.

8

"Because the only friends you'll have are the ones you buy!"

I tried to smile, but there was a lot of truth in Jack's words. A spook worked and lived alone.

"Oh, Jack! Don't be cruel!" Ellie scolded.

"It was only a joke," Jack replied, as if he couldn't understand why Ellie was making so much fuss.

But Ellie was looking at me rather than Jack, and I saw her face suddenly drop. "Oh, Tom!" she said. "This means that you won't be here when the baby's born. . . ."

She looked really disappointed, and it made me feel sad that I wouldn't be at home to see my new niece. Mam had said that Ellie's baby was going to be a girl, and she was never wrong about things like that.

"I'll come back and visit just as soon as I can," I promised.

Ellie tried to smile, and Jack came up and rested his arm across my shoulders. "You'll always have your family," he said. "We'll always be here if you need us."

❂ ❂ ❂

9

An hour later I sat down to supper, knowing that I'd be gone in the morning. Dad said grace as he did every evening and we all muttered "amen" except Mam. She just stared down at her food as usual, waiting politely until it was over. As the prayer ended, Mam gave me a little smile. It was a warm, special smile, and I don't think anyone else noticed. It made me feel better.

The fire was still burning in the grate, filling the kitchen with warmth. At the center of our large wooden table was a brass candlestick, which had been polished until you could see your face in it. The candle was made of beeswax and was expensive, but Mam wouldn't allow tallow in the kitchen because of the smell. Dad made most of the decisions on the farm, but in some things she always got her own way.

As we tucked into our big plates of steaming hot pot, it struck me how old Dad looked tonight—old and tired— and there was an expression that flickered across his face from time to time, a hint of sadness. But he brightened up a bit when he and Jack started discussing the price of pork and whether or not it was the right time to send for the pig butcher.

"Better to wait another month or so," Dad said. "The price is sure to go higher."

Jack shook his head and they began to argue. It was a friendly argument, the kind families often have, and I could tell that Dad was enjoying it. I didn't join in, though. All that was over for me. As Dad had told me, I was finished with farming.

Mam and Ellie were chuckling together softly. I tried to catch what they were saying, but by now Jack was in full flow, his voice getting louder and louder. When Mam glanced across at him, I could tell she'd had enough of his noise.

Oblivious to Mam's glances, and continuing to argue loudly, Jack reached across for the salt cellar and accidentally knocked it over, spilling a small cone of salt on the tabletop. Straightaway he took a pinch and threw it back over his left shoulder. It is an old County superstition. By doing that you were supposed to ward off the bad luck you'd earned by spilling it.

"Jack, you don't need any salt on that anyway," Mam scolded. "It spoils a good hot pot and is an insult to the cook!"

"Sorry, Mam," Jack apologized. "You're right. It's perfect just as it is."

She gave him a smile, then nodded toward me. "Anyway, nobody's taking any notice of Tom. That's no way to treat him on his last night at home."

"I'm all right, Mam," I told her. "I'm happy just to sit here and listen."

Mam nodded. "Well, I've got a few things to say to you. After supper stay down in the kitchen, and we'll have a little talk."

So after Jack, Ellie, and Dad had gone up to bed, I sat in a chair by the fire and waited patiently to hear what Mam had to say.

Mam wasn't a woman who made a lot of fuss; at first she didn't say much, apart from explaining what she was wrapping up for me: a spare pair of trousers, three shirts, and two pairs of good socks that had only been darned once each.

I stared into the embers of the fire, tapping my feet on the flags, while Mam drew up her rocking chair and positioned it so that she was facing directly toward me. Her black hair was streaked with a few strands of gray, but apart from that she looked much the same as she had when I was just a toddler, hardly up to her knees. Her eyes were still bright, and but for her pale skin, she looked a picture of health.

"This is the last time we'll get to talk together for a long while," she said. "It's a big step leaving home and starting out on your own. So if there's anything you need to say, anything you need to ask, now's the time to do it."

I couldn't think of a single question. In fact I couldn't even think. Hearing her say all that had started tears pricking behind my eyes.

The silence went on for quite a while. All that could be heard was my feet tap-tapping on the flags. Finally Mam gave a little sigh. "What's wrong?" she asked. "Has the cat got your tongue?"

I shrugged.

"Stop fidgeting, Tom, and concentrate on what I'm saying," Mam warned. "First of all, are you looking forward to tomorrow and starting your new job?"

"I'm not sure, Mam," I told her, remembering Jack's joke about having to buy friends. "Nobody wants to go anywhere near a spook. I'll have no friends. I'll be lonely all the time."

"It won't be as bad as you think," Mam said. "You'll have your master to talk to. He'll be your teacher, and no doubt he'll eventually become your friend. And you'll be busy all the time. Busy learning new things. You'll have no time to feel lonely. Don't you find the whole thing new and exciting?"

"It's exciting, but the job scares me. I want to do it, but I don't know if I can. One part of me wants to travel and see places, but it'll be hard not to live here anymore. I'll miss you all. I'll miss being at home."

"You can't stay here," Mam said. "Your dad's getting too old to work, and come next winter he's handing the farm over to Jack. Ellie will be having her baby soon, no doubt the first of many; eventually there won't be room for you here. No, you'd better get used to it before that happens. You can't come home."

Her voice seemed cold and a little sharp, and to hear her speak to me like that drove a pain deep into my chest and throat so that I could hardly breathe.

I just wanted to go to bed then, but she had a lot to say. I'd rarely heard her use so many words all in one go.

"You have a job to do and you're going to do it," she said sternly. "And not only do it; you're going to do it well. I married your dad because he was a seventh son. And I bore him six sons so that I could have you. Seven times seven, you are, and you have the gift. Your new master's still strong, but he's some way past his best, and his time is finally coming to an end.

"For nearly sixty years he's walked the County lines doing his duty. Doing what has to be done. Soon it'll be your turn. And if you won't do it, then who will? Who'll look after the ordinary folk? Who'll keep them from harm? Who'll make the farms, villages, and towns safe so that women and children can walk the streets and lanes free from fear?"

I didn't know what to say, and I couldn't look her in the eye. I just fought to hold back the tears.

"I love everyone in this house," she said, her voice softening, "but in the whole wide County, you're the only person who's really like me. As yet, you're just a boy who's still got a lot of growing to do, but you're the seventh son of a seventh son. You've the gift and the strength to do what has to be done. I know you're going to make me proud of you.

"Well, now," Mam said, coming to her feet, "I'm glad that we've got that sorted out. Now off to bed with you. It's a big day tomorrow, and you want to be at your best."

She gave me a hug and a warm smile, and I tried really hard to be cheerful and smile back, but once up in my bedroom I sat on the edge of my bed just staring vacantly and thinking about what Mam had told me.

My mam is well respected in the neighborhood. She

knows more about plants and medicines than the local doctor, and when there is a problem with delivering a baby, the midwife always sends for her. Mam is an expert on what she calls breech births. Sometimes a baby tries to get born feet first, but my mother is good at turning them while they are still in the womb. Dozens of women in the County owe their lives to her.

Anyway, that was what my dad always said, but Mam was modest and she never mentioned things like that. She just got on with what had to be done, and I knew that's what she expected of me. So I wanted to make her proud.

But could she really mean that she'd only married my dad and had my six brothers so she could give birth to me? It didn't seem possible.

After thinking things through, I went across to the window and sat in the old wicker chair for a few minutes, staring through the window, which faced north.

The moon was shining, bathing everything in its silver light. I could see across the farmyard, beyond the two hay fields and the north pasture, right to the boundary of our farm, which ended halfway up Hangman's Hill. I liked the view. I liked Hangman's Hill, from a distance. I liked the way it was the farthest thing you could see.

For years this had been my routine before climbing into bed each night. I used to stare at that hill and imagine what was on the other side. I knew that it was really just more fields and then, two miles farther on, what passed for the local village—half a dozen houses, a small church, and an even smaller school—but my imagination conjured up other things. Sometimes I imagined high cliffs with an ocean beyond, or maybe a forest or a great city with tall towers and twinkling lights.

But now, as I gazed at the hill, I remembered my fear as well. Yes, it was fine from a distance, but it wasn't a place I'd ever wanted to get close to. Hangman's Hill, as you might have guessed, didn't get its name for nothing.

Three generations earlier, a war had raged over the whole land, and the men of the County had played their part. It had been that worst of all wars, a bitter civil war where families had been divided and where sometimes brother had even fought brother.

In the last winter of the war there'd been a big battle a mile or so to the north, just on the outskirts of the village. When it was finally over, the winning army had brought their prisoners to this hill and hanged them from the trees on its northern slope. They'd hanged some of their own men, too, for what they claimed was cowardice in the face of the enemy, but there was another version of that tale. It was said that some of these men had refused to fight people they considered to be neighbors.

Even Jack never liked working close to that boundary fence, and the dogs wouldn't go more than a few feet into the wood. As for me, because I can sense things that others can't, I couldn't even work in the north pasture. You see, from there I could hear them. I could hear the ropes creaking and the branches groaning under their weight. I could hear the dead, strangling and choking on the other side of the hill.

Mam had said that we were like each other. Well, she was certainly like me in one way: I knew she could also see things that others couldn't. One winter, when I was very young and all my brothers lived at home, the noises from the hill got so bad at night that I could even hear them from my bedroom. My brothers didn't hear a thing, but I did, and I couldn't sleep. Mam came to my room every time I called, even though she had to be up at the crack of dawn to do her chores.

Finally she said she was going to sort it out, and one night she climbed Hangman's Hill alone and went up into the trees. When she came back, everything was quiet, and it stayed like that for months afterward.

So there was one way in which we weren't alike.

Mam was a lot braver than I was.

CHAPTER II
ON THE ROAD

I WAS up an hour before dawn, but Mam was already in the kitchen, cooking my favorite breakfast, bacon and eggs.

Dad came downstairs while I was mopping the plate with my last slice of bread. As we said good-bye, he pulled something from his pocket and placed it in my hands. It was the small tinderbox that had belonged to his own dad and to his granddad before that. One of his favorite possessions.

"I want you to have this, son," he said. "It might come in useful in your new job. And come back and see us soon. Just because you've left home, it doesn't mean that you can't come back and visit."

"It's time to go, son," Mam said, walking across to give me a final hug. "He's at the gate. Don't keep him waiting."

We were a family that didn't like too much fuss, and as we'd already said our good-byes, I walked out into the yard alone.

The Spook was on the other side of the gate, a dark silhouette against the gray dawn light. His hood was up and he was standing straight and tall, his staff in his left hand. I walked toward him, carrying my small bundle of possessions, feeling very nervous.

To my surprise, the Spook opened the gate and came into the yard. "Well, lad," he said, "follow me! We might as well start the way we mean to go on."

Instead of heading for the road, he led the way north,

directly toward Hangman's Hill, and soon we were cross-
ing the north pasture, my heart already starting to
thump. When we reached the boundary fence, the Spook
climbed over with the ease of a man half his age, but I
froze. As I rested my hands against the top edge of the
fence, I could already hear the sounds of the trees creaking, their branches bent and bowed under the weight of
the hanging men.

"What's the matter, lad?" asked the Spook, turning to
look back at me. "If you're frightened of something on
your own doorstep, you'll be of little use to me."

I took a deep breath and clambered over the fence. We
trudged upward, the dawn light darkening as we moved
up into the gloom of the trees. The higher we climbed, the
colder it seemed to get, and soon I was shivering. It was
the kind of cold that gives you goose pimples and makes
the hair on the back of your neck start to rise. It was a
warning that something wasn't quite right. I'd felt it
before when something had come close that didn't belong
in this world.

Once we'd reached the summit of the hill, I could see them below me. There had to be a hundred at least, sometimes two or three hanging from the same tree, wearing soldiers' uniforms with broad leather belts and big boots. Their hands were tied behind their backs and all of them behaved differently. Some struggled desperately so that the branch above them bounced and jerked, while others were just spinning slowly on the end of the rope, pointing first one way, then the other.

As I watched, I suddenly felt a strong wind on my face, a wind so cold and fierce that it couldn't have been natural. The trees bowed low, and their leaves shriveled and began to fall. Within moments, all the branches were bare. When the wind had eased, the Spook put his hand on my shoulder and guided me nearer to the hanging men. We stopped just feet away from the nearest.

"Look at him," said the Spook. "What do you see?"

"A dead soldier," I replied, my voice beginning to wobble.

"How old does he look?"

"Seventeen at the most."

"Good. Well done, lad. Now, tell me, do you still feel scared?"

"A bit. I don't like being so close to him."

"Why? There's nothing to be afraid of. Nothing that can hurt you. Think about what it must have been like for him. Concentrate on him rather than yourself. How must he have felt? What would be the worst thing?"

I tried to put myself in the soldier's place and imagine how it must have been to die like that. The pain and the struggle for breath would have been terrible. But there might have been something even worse. . . .

"He'd have known he was dying and that he'd never be able to go home again. That he'd never see his family again," I told the Spook.

With those words a wave of sadness washed over me. Then, even as that happened, the hanging men slowly began to disappear, until we were alone on the hillside and the leaves were back on the trees.

"How do you feel now? Still afraid?"

I shook my head. "No," I said. "I just feel sad."

"Well done, lad. You're learning. We're the seventh sons of seventh sons, and we have the gift of seeing things that others can't. But that gift can sometimes be a curse. If we're afraid, sometimes there are things that can feed on that fear. Fear makes it worse for us. The trick is to concentrate on what you can see and stop thinking about yourself. It works every time.

"It was a terrible sight, lad, but they're just ghasts," continued the Spook. "There's nothing much we can do about them, and they'll just fade away in their own time. In a hundred years or so there'll be nothing left."

I felt like telling him that Mam did something about them once, but I didn't. To contradict him would have gotten us off to a bad start.

"Now if they were ghosts, that would be different," said the Spook. "You can talk to ghosts and tell them what's what. Just making them realize that they're dead is a great kindness and an important step in getting them to move on. Usually a ghost is a bewildered spirit trapped on this earth but not knowing what's happened. So often they're in torment. Then again, others are here with a definite purpose, and they might have things to tell you. But a ghast is just a fragment of a soul that's gone on to better things. That's what these are, lad. Just ghasts. You saw the trees change?"

"The leaves fell and it was winter."

"Well, the leaves are back now. So you were just looking at something from the past. Just a reminder of the evil things that sometimes happen on this earth. Usually, if you're brave, they can't see you and they don't feel anything. A ghast is just like a reflection in a pond that stays behind when its owner has moved on. Understand what I'm saying?"

I nodded.

"Right, so that's one thing sorted out. We'll be dealing with the dead from time to time, so you might as well get used to them. Anyway, let's get started. We've quite a way to go. Here, from now on you'll be carrying this."

The Spook handed me his big leather bag and, without a backward glance, headed back up the hill. I followed him over its crest, then down through the trees toward the road, which was a distant gray scar meandering its way south through the green and brown patchwork of fields.

"Done much traveling, lad?" the Spook called back over his shoulder. "Seen much of the County?"

I told him I'd never been more than six miles from my dad's farm. Going to the local market was the most traveling I'd ever done.

The Spook muttered something under his breath and shook his head; I could tell that he wasn't best pleased by my answer.

"Well, your travels start today," he said. "We're heading south toward a village called Horshaw. It's just over fifteen miles as the crow flies, and we have to be there before dark."

I'd heard of Horshaw. It was a pit village and had the largest coal yards in the County, holding the output of dozens of surrounding mines. I'd never expected to go there, and I wondered what the Spook's business could be in a place like that.

He walked at a furious pace, taking big, effortless strides. Soon I was struggling to keep up; as well as carrying my own small bundle of clothes and other belongings, I now had his bag, which seemed to be getting heavier by the minute. Then, just to make things worse, it started to rain.

About an hour before noon, the Spook came to a sudden halt. He turned round and stared hard at me. By then I was about ten paces behind. My feet were hurting and I'd already developed a slight limp. The road was little more than a track that was quickly turning to mud. Just as I caught up with him, I stubbed my toe, slipped, and almost lost my balance.

He tutted. "Feeling dizzy, lad?" he asked.

I shook my head. I wanted to give my arm a rest, but it didn't seem right to put his bag down in the mud.

"That's good," said the Spook with a faint smile, the rain dripping from the edge of his hood down onto his beard. "Never trust a man who's dizzy. That's something well worth remembering."

"I'm not dizzy," I protested.

"No?" asked the Spook, raising his bushy eyebrows. "Then it must be your boots. They won't be much use in this job."

My boots were the same as my dad's and Jack's, sturdy enough and suitable for the mud and muck of the farmyard, but the kind that needed a lot of getting used to. A new pair usually cost you a fortnight's blisters before your feet got bedded in.

I looked down at the Spook's. They were made of strong, good-quality leather, and they had extra-thick soles. They must have cost a fortune, but I suppose that for someone who did a lot of walking, they were worth every penny. They flexed as he walked, and I just knew that they'd been comfortable from the very first moment he pulled them on.

"Good boots are important in this job," said the Spook. "We depend on neither man nor beast to get us where we need to go. If you rely on your own two good legs, then they won't let you down. So if I finally decide to take you on, I'll get you a pair of boots just like mine. Until then, you'll just have to manage as best you can."

At noon we halted for a short break, sheltering from the rain in an abandoned cattle shed. The Spook took a piece of cloth out of his pocket and unwrapped it, revealing a large lump of yellow cheese.

He broke off a bit and handed it to me. I'd seen worse and I was hungry, so I wolfed it down. The Spook only ate a small piece himself before wrapping the rest up again and stuffing it back into his pocket.

Once out of the rain, he'd pulled his hood back, so I now had the chance to look at him properly for the first time. Apart from the full beard and the hangman's eyes, his most noticeable feature was his nose, which was grim and sharp, with a curve to it that suggested a bird's beak. The mouth, when closed, was almost hidden by that mustache and beard. The beard itself had looked gray at first glance, but when I looked closer, trying to be as casual as possible so that he wouldn't notice, I saw that most of the colors of the rainbow seemed to be sprouting there. There were shades of red, black, brown, and, obviously, lots of gray, but as I came to realize later, it all depended on the light.

"Weak jaw, weak character," my dad always used to say, and he also believed that some men wore beards just to hide that fact. Looking at the Spook, though, you could see despite the beard that his jaw was long, and when he opened his mouth he revealed yellow teeth that were very sharp and more suited to gnawing on red meat than nibbling at cheese.

With a shiver, I suddenly realized that he reminded me of a wolf. And it wasn't just the way he looked. He was a kind of predator because he hunted the dark; living merely on nibbles of cheese would make him always hungry and mean. If I completed my apprenticeship, I'd end up just like him.

"You still hungry, lad?" he asked, his green eyes boring hard into my own until I started to feel a bit dizzy.

I was soaked to the skin and my feet were hurting, but most of all I was hungry. So I nodded, thinking he might offer me some more, but he just shook his head and muttered something to himself. Then, once again, he looked at me sharply.

"Hunger's something you're going to have to get used to," he said. "We don't eat much when we're working, and if the job's very difficult, we don't eat anything at all until afterward. Fasting's the safest thing because it makes us less vulnerable to the dark. It makes us stronger. So you might as well start practicing now, because when we get to Horshaw, I'm going to give you a little test. You're going to spend a night in a haunted house. And you're going to do it alone. That'll show me what you're really made of!"

CHAPTER III
NUMBER THIRTEEN WATERY LANE

WE reached Horshaw as a church bell began to chime in the distance. It was seven o'clock and starting to get dark. A heavy drizzle blew straight into our faces, but there was still enough light for me to judge that this wasn't a place I ever wanted to live in and that even a short visit would be best avoided.

Horshaw was a black smear against the green fields, a grim, ugly little place with about two dozen rows of mean back-to-back houses huddling together mainly on the southern slope of a damp, bleak hillside. The whole area was riddled with mines, and Horshaw was at its center. High above the village was a large slag heap, which marked the entrance to a mine. Behind the slag heap were the coal yards, which stored enough fuel to keep the biggest towns in the County warm through even the longest of winters.

Soon we were walking down through the narrow, cobbled streets, keeping pressed close to the grimy walls to make way for carts heaped with black lumps of coal, wet and gleaming with rain. The huge shire horses that pulled them were straining against their loads, hooves slipping on the shiny cobbles.

There were few people about, but lace curtains twitched as we passed, and once we met a group of dour-faced miners who were trudging up the hill to begin their night shift. They'd been talking in loud voices but suddenly fell silent and moved into a single column to pass us, keeping to the far side of the street. One of them actually made the sign of the cross.

"Get used to it, lad," growled the Spook. "We're needed but rarely welcomed, and some places are worse than others."

Finally we turned a corner into the lowest and meanest street of all. Nobody lived there—you could tell that right away. For one thing, some of the windows were broken and others were boarded up, and although it was almost dark, no lights were showing. At one end of the street was an abandoned corn merchant's warehouse, two huge wooden doors gaping open and hanging from their rusty hinges.

The Spook halted outside the very last house. It was the one on the corner closest to the warehouse, the only house in the street to have a number. That number was crafted out of metal and nailed to the door. It was thirteen, the worst and unluckiest of all numbers, and directly above, there was a street sign high on the wall, hanging from a single rusty rivet and pointing almost vertically toward the cobbles. It said WATERY LANE.

This house did have windowpanes, but the lace curtains were yellow and hung with cobwebs. This must be the haunted house my master had warned me about.

The Spook pulled a key from his pocket, unlocked the door, and led the way into the darkness within. At first I was just glad to be out of the drizzle, but when he lit a candle and positioned it on the floor near the middle of the small front room, I knew that I'd be more comfortable in an abandoned cowshed. There wasn't a single item of furniture to be seen, just a bare flagged floor and a heap of dirty straw under the window. The room was damp, too, the air very dank and cold, and by the light of the flickering candle I could see my breath steaming.

What I saw was bad enough, but what he said was even worse.

"Well, lad, I've got business to attend to so I'll be off, but I'll be back later. Know what you have to do?"

"No, sir," I replied, watching the flickering candle,

worried that it might go out at any second.

"Well, it's what I told you earlier. Weren't you listening? You need to be alert, not dreaming. Anyway, it's nothing very difficult," he explained, scratching at his beard as if there was something crawling about in it. "You just have to spend the night here alone. I bring all my new apprentices to this old house on their first night so I can find out what they're made of. Oh, but there's one thing I haven't told you. At midnight I'll expect you to go down into the cellar and face whatever it is that's lurking there. Cope with that and you're well on your way to being taken on permanently. Any questions?"

I had questions all right, but I was too scared to hear the answers. So I just shook my head and tried to keep my top lip from trembling.

"How will you know when it's midnight?" he asked.

I shrugged. I was pretty good at guessing the time from the position of the sun or the stars, and if I ever woke in the middle of the night, I almost always knew exactly what time it was, but here I wasn't so sure. In some places time seems to move more slowly, and I had a feeling that this old house would be one of them.

Suddenly I remembered the church clock. "It's just gone seven," I said. "I'll listen for twelve chimes."

"Well, at least you're awake now," the Spook said with a little smile. "When the clock strikes twelve, take the stub of the candle and use it to find your way down to the cellar. Until then, sleep if you can manage it. Now listen carefully—there are three important things to remember. Don't open the front door to anyone, no matter how hard they knock, and don't be late going down to the cellar."

He took a step toward the front door.

"What's the third thing?" I called out at the very last moment.

"The candle, lad. Whatever else you do, don't let it go out."

Then he was gone, closing the door behind him, and I was all alone. Cautiously I picked up the candle, walked to the kitchen door, and peered inside. It was empty of everything but a stone sink. The back door was closed, but the wind still wailed beneath it. There were two other doors on the right. One was open, and I could see the bare wooden stairs that led to the bedrooms above. The other one, that closest to me, was closed.

Something about that closed door made me uneasy, but I decided to take a quick look. Nervously I gripped the handle and tugged at the door. It was hard to shift, and for a moment I had a creepy feeling that somebody was holding it closed on the other side. When I tugged even harder, it opened with a jerk, making me lose my balance. I staggered back a couple of steps and almost dropped the candle.

Stone steps led down into the darkness; they were black with coal dust. They curved away to the left so I couldn't see right down into the cellar, but a cold draft came up them, making the candle flame dance and flicker. I closed the door quickly and went back into the front room, closing the kitchen door, too.

I put the candle down carefully in the corner farthest away from the door and window. Once I was satisfied that it wouldn't fall over, I looked for a place on the floor where I could sleep. There wasn't much choice. I certainly wasn't sleeping on the damp straw, so I settled down in the center of the room.

The flags were hard and cold, but I closed my eyes. Once asleep, I'd be away from that grim old house, and I felt pretty confident that I'd wake just before midnight.

Usually I get to sleep easily, but this was different. I kept shivering with cold, and the wind was beginning to rattle the windowpanes. There were also rustlings and patterings coming from the walls. Just mice, I kept telling myself. We were certainly used to them on the farm. But then, suddenly, there came a disturbing new sound from down below in the depths of the dark cellar.

At first it was faint, making me strain my ears, but gradually it grew until I was in no doubt about what I could hear. Down in the cellar, something was happening that shouldn't be happening. Someone was digging rhythmically, turning heavy earth with a sharp metal spade. First came the grind of the metal edge striking a stony surface, followed by a soft, squelching, sucking sound as the spade pushed deep into heavy clay and tore it free from the earth.

This went on for several minutes until the noise stopped as suddenly as it had begun. All was quiet. Even the mice stopped their pattering. It was as if the house and everything in it were holding their breath. I know I was.

The silence ended with a resounding thump. Then a whole series of thumps, definite in rhythm. Thumps that were getting louder. And louder. And closer . . .

Someone was climbing the stairs from the cellar.

I snatched up the candle and shrank into the farthest corner. *Thump, thump,* nearer and nearer, came the sound of heavy boots. Who could have been digging down there in the darkness? Who could be climbing the stairs now?

But maybe it wasn't a question of *who* was climbing the stairs. Maybe it was a question of *what*.

I heard the cellar door open and the thump of boots in the kitchen. I pressed myself back into the corner, trying to make myself small, waiting for the kitchen door to open.

And open it did, very slowly, with a loud creak. Something stepped into the room. I felt coldness then. Real coldness. The kind of coldness that told me something was close that didn't belong on this earth. It was like the coldness of Hangman's Hill, only far, far worse.

I lifted the candle, its flame flickering eerie shadows that danced up the walls and onto the ceiling.

"Who's there?" I asked. "Who's there?" My voice trembled even more than the hand holding the candle.

There was no answer. Even the wind outside had fallen silent.

"Who's there?" I called out again.

Again no reply, but invisible boots grated on the flags as they stepped toward me. Nearer and nearer they came, and now I could hear breathing. Something big was breathing heavily. It sounded like a huge carthorse that had just pulled a heavy load up a steep hill.

At the very last moment the footsteps veered away

from me and halted close to the window. I was holding my breath, and the thing by the window seemed to be breathing for both of us, drawing great gulps of air into its lungs as if it could never get enough.

Just when I could stand it no longer, it gave a huge sigh that sounded weary and sad at the same time, and the invisible boots grated on the flags once more, heavy steps that moved away from the window, back toward the door. When they began to thump their way down the cellar steps, I was finally able to breathe again.

My heart began to slow, my hands stopped shaking, and gradually I calmed down. I had to pull myself together. I'd been scared, but if that was the worst that was going to happen tonight, I'd gotten through it, passed my first test. I was going to be the Spook's apprentice, so I'd have to get used to places like this haunted house. It went with the job.

After about five minutes or so I began to feel better. I even thought about making another attempt to get to sleep, but as my dad sometimes says, "There's no rest for the wicked." Well, I don't know what I'd done wrong, but there was a sudden new sound to disturb me.

It was faint and distant at first — something knocking on a door. There was a pause, and then it happened again. Three distinct raps, but a little nearer this time. Another pause and three more raps.

It didn't take me long to work it out. Something was rapping hard on each door in the street, moving nearer and nearer to number thirteen. When it finally came to the haunted house, the three raps on the front door were loud enough to wake the dead. Would the thing in the cellar climb the steps to answer that summons? I felt trapped between the two: something outside wanting to get in; something below that wanted to be free.

And then, suddenly, it was all right. A voice called to me from the other side of the front door, a voice I recognized.

"Tom! Tom! Open the door! Let me in!"

It was Mam. I was so glad to hear her that I rushed to the front door without thinking. It was raining outside and she'd be getting wet.

"Quickly, Tom, quickly!" Mam called. "Don't keep me waiting."

I was actually lifting the latch to open it when I remembered the Spook's warning: *"Don't open the front door to anyone, no matter how hard they knock."*

But how could I leave Mam out there in the dark?

"Come on, Tom! Let me in!" the voice called again.

Remembering what the Spook had said, I took a deep breath and tried to think. Common sense told me it couldn't be her. Why would she have followed me all this way? How would she have known where we were going? Mam wouldn't have traveled alone either. My dad or Jack would have come with her.

No, it was a something else waiting outside. Something without hands that could still rap on the door. Something without feet that could still stand on the pavement.

The knocking started to get louder.

"Please let me in, Tom," pleaded the voice. "How can you be so hard and cruel? I'm cold, wet, and tired."

Eventually it began to cry, and then I knew for certain that it couldn't possibly be Mam. Mam was strong. Mam never cried no matter how bad things got.

After a few moments the sounds faded and stopped altogether. I lay down on the floor and tried to sleep again. I kept turning over, first one way and then the other, but try as I might, I couldn't get to sleep. The wind began to rattle the windowpanes even louder, and on every hour and half hour the church clock chimed, moving me closer to midnight.

The nearer the time came for me to go down the cellar steps, the more nervous I became. I did want to pass the Spook's test, but, oh, how I longed to be back home in my nice, safe, warm bed.

And then, just after the clock had given a single chime—half past eleven—the digging began again. . . .

Once more I heard the slow *thump, thump* of heavy boots coming up the steps from the cellar; once more the door opened and the invisible boots stepped into the front room. By now the only bit of me that was moving was my heart, which pounded so hard it seemed about to break my ribs. But this time the boots didn't veer away in the direction of the window. They kept coming. *Thump! Thump! Thump!* Coming straight toward me.

I felt myself being lifted roughly by the hair and skin at the nape of my neck, just like a mother cat carries her kittens. Then an invisible arm wrapped itself around my body, pinning my arms to my sides. I tried to suck in a breath, but it was impossible. My chest was being crushed.

I was being carried toward the cellar door. I couldn't see what was carrying me, but I could hear its wheezing breath and I struggled in a panic, because somehow I knew exactly what was going to happen. Somehow I knew why there'd been the sound of digging from below. I was going to be carried down the cellar steps into the darkness, and I knew that a grave was waiting for me down there. I was going to be buried alive.

I was terrified and tried to cry out, but it was worse than just being held in a tight grip. I was paralyzed and couldn't move a muscle.

Suddenly I was falling. . . .

I found myself on all fours, staring at the open door to the cellar, just inches from the top step. In a panic, my heart thumping too fast to count the beats, I lurched to my feet and slammed the cellar door shut. Still trembling, I went back into the front room to find that one of the Spook's three rules had been broken.

The candle had gone out.

As I walked toward the window, a sudden flash of light illuminated the room, followed by a loud crash of thunder almost directly overhead. Rain squalled against the house, rattling the windows and making the front door creak and groan as if something were trying to get in.

I stared out miserably for a few minutes, watching the flashes of lightning. It was a bad night, but even though lightning scared me, I would have given anything to be out there walking the streets; anything to have avoided going down into that cellar.

In the distance the church clock began to chime. I

counted the chimes, and there were exactly twelve. Now I had to face what was in the cellar.

It was then, as lightning lit the room again, that I noticed the large footprints on the floor. At first I thought they'd been made by the Spook, but they were black, as if the huge boots that made them had been covered with coal dust. They came from the direction of the kitchen door, went almost to the window, and then turned and went back the way they'd come. Back to the cellar. Down into the dark where I had to go!

Forcing myself forward, I searched the floor with my hand for the stub of the candle. Then I scrabbled around for my small bundle of clothes. Wrapped in the center of it was the tinderbox that Dad had given me.

Fumbling in the dark, I shook the small pile of tinder out onto the floor and used the stone and metal to strike up sparks. I kindled that little pile of wood until it burst into flame, just long enough to light the candle. Little had Dad known that his gift would prove so useful so soon.

As I opened the cellar door, there was another flash of

lightning and a sudden crash of thunder that shook the whole house and rumbled down the steps ahead of me. I descended into the cellar, my hand trembling and the candle stub dancing till strange shadows flickered against the wall.

I didn't want to go down there, but if I failed the Spook's test, I'd probably be on my way back home as soon as it came light. I imagined my shame at having to tell Mam what had happened.

Eight steps and I was turning the corner so that the cellar was in view. It wasn't a big cellar, but it had dark shadows in the corners that the candlelight couldn't quite reach, and there were spiders' webs hanging from the ceiling in frail, mucky curtains. Small pieces of coal and large wooden crates were scattered across the earthen floor, and there was an old wooden table next to a big beer barrel. I stepped around the beer barrel and noticed something in the far corner. Something just behind some crates that scared me so much I almost dropped the candle.

It was a dark shape, almost like a bundle of rags, and it was making a noise. A faint, rhythmical sound, like breathing.

I took a step toward the rags; then another, using all my willpower to make my legs move. It was then, as I got so close that I could have touched it, that the thing suddenly grew. From a shadow on the floor it reared up before me until it was three or four times bigger.

I almost ran. It was tall, dark, hooded, and terrifying, with green, glittering eyes.

Only then did I notice the staff that it was holding in its left hand.

"What kept you?" demanded the Spook. "You're nearly five minutes late!"

CHAPTER IV
THE LETTER

X
Gregory

"I LIVED in this house as a child," said the Spook, "and I saw things that would make your big toes curl, but I was the only one who could, and my dad used to beat me for telling lies. Something used to climb up out of the cellar. It would have been the same for you. Am I right?"

I nodded.

· 57 ·

"Well, it's nothing to worry about, lad. It's just another ghast, a fragment of a troubled soul that's gone on to better things. Without leaving the bad part of himself behind, he'd have been stuck here forever."

"What did he do?" I asked, my voice echoing back slightly from the ceiling.

The Spook shook his head sadly. "He was a miner whose lungs were so diseased that he couldn't work anymore. He spent his days and nights coughing and struggling for breath, and his poor wife kept them both. She worked in a bakery, but sadly for both of them, she was a very pretty woman, and some pretty women can't be trusted.

"To make it worse, he was a jealous man and his illness made him bitter. One evening she was very late home from work and he kept going to the window, pacing backward and forward, getting more and more angry because he thought she was with another man.

"When she finally came in, he was in such a rage that he broke her head open with a big lump of coal. Then he left her there, dying on the flags, and went down into the cellar to dig a grave. She was still alive when he came back, but she couldn't move and couldn't even cry out. That's the terror that comes to us, because it's how she felt as he picked her up and carried her down into the darkness of the cellar. She'd heard him digging. She knew what he was going to do.

"Later that night he killed himself. It's a sad story, but although they're at peace now, his ghast's still here and so are her final memories, both strong enough to torment folks like us. We see things that others can't, which is both a blessing and a curse. It's a very useful thing in our trade, though."

I shuddered. I felt sorry for the poor wife who'd been murdered, and I felt sorry for the miner who'd killed her. I even felt sorry for the Spook. Imagine having to spend your childhood in a house like this.

I looked down at the candle, which I'd placed in the middle of the table. It was almost burned down and the flame was starting its last flickering dance, but the Spook didn't show any sign of wanting to go back upstairs. I didn't like the shadows on his face. It looked as if it were gradually changing, as if he were growing a snout or something.

"Do you know how I overcame my fear?" he asked.

"No, sir."

"One night I was so terrified that I screamed out before I could stop myself. I woke everybody up, and in a rage my father lifted me up by the scruff of my neck and carried me down the steps into this cellar. Then he got a hammer and nailed the door shut behind me.

"I wasn't very old. Probably seven at the most. I climbed back up the steps and, screaming fit to burst, scratched and banged at the door. But my father was a hard man, and he left me all alone in the dark and I had to stay there for hours, until long after dawn. After a bit, I calmed down, and do you know what I did then?"

I shook my head, trying not to look at his face. His eyes were glittering very brightly, and he looked more like a wolf than ever.

"I walked down the steps and sat there in this cellar in the darkness. Then I took three deep breaths, and I faced my fear. I faced the darkness itself, which is the most terrifying thing of all, especially for people like us, because things come to us in the dark. They seek us out with whispers and take shapes that only our eyes can see. But I did it, and when I left this cellar the worst was over."

At that moment the candle guttered and then went out, plunging us into absolute darkness.

"This is it, lad," the Spook said. "There's just you, me, and the dark. Can you stand it? Are you fit to be my apprentice?"

His voice sounded different, sort of deeper and strange. I imagined him on all fours by now, wolf hair covering his face, his teeth growing longer. I was trembling and couldn't speak until I'd taken my third deep breath. Only then did I give him my answer. It was something my dad always said when he had to do something unpleasant or difficult.

"Someone has to do it," I said. "So it might as well be me."

The Spook must have thought that was funny, because his laughter filled the whole cellar before rumbling up the steps to meet the next peal of thunder, which was on its way down.

"Nearly thirteen years ago," said the Spook, "a sealed letter was sent to me. It was short and to the point and it was written in Greek. Your mother sent it. Do you know what it said?"

"No," I said quietly, wondering what was coming next.

" 'I've just given birth to a baby boy,' she wrote, 'and he's the seventh son of a seventh son. His name is Thomas J. Ward, and he's my gift to the County. When he's old enough we'll send you word. Train him well. He'll be the best apprentice you've ever had, and he'll also be your last.' "

"We don't use magic, lad," the Spook said, his voice hardly more than a whisper in the darkness. "The main tools of our trade are common sense, courage, and the keeping of accurate records, so we can learn from the past. Above all, we don't believe in prophecy. We don't believe that the future is fixed. So if what your mother wrote comes true, then it's because *we* make it come true. Do you understand?"

There was an edge of anger in his voice, but I knew it wasn't directed at me, so I just nodded into the darkness.

"As for being your mother's gift to the County, every single one of my apprentices was the seventh son of a seventh son. So don't you start thinking you're anything special. You've a lot of study and hard work ahead of you.

"Family can be a nuisance," the Spook went on after a pause, his voice softer, the anger gone. "I've only got two brothers left now. One's a locksmith and we get on all right, but the other one hasn't spoken to me for well over forty years, though he still lives here in Horshaw."

By the time we left the house, the storm had blown itself out and the moon was visible. As the Spook closed the front door, I noticed for the first time what had been carved there in the wood.

Gregory

The Spook nodded toward it. "I use signs like this to warn others who've the skill to read them or sometimes just to jog my own memory. You'll recognize the Greek letter gamma. It's the sign for either a ghost or a ghast. The cross on the lower right is the Roman numeral for ten, which is the lowest grading of all. Anything above six is just a ghast. There's nothing in that house that can harm you, not if you're brave. Remember, the dark feeds on fear. Be brave and there's nothing much a ghast can do."

If only I'd known that to begin with!

"Buck up, lad," said the Spook. "Your face is nearly down in your boots! Well, maybe this'll cheer you up." He pulled the lump of yellow cheese out of his pocket, broke off a small piece, and handed it to me. "Chew on this," he said, "but don't swallow it all at once."

I followed him down the cobbled street. The air was damp, but at least it wasn't raining, and to the west the clouds looked like lamb's wool against the sky and were starting to tear and break up into ragged strips.

We left the village and continued south. Right on its edge, where the cobbled street became a muddy lane, there was a small church. It looked neglected—there were slates missing off the roof and paint peeling from the main door. We'd hardly seen anyone since leaving the house, but there was an old man standing in the doorway. His hair was white and it was lank, greasy, and unkempt.

His dark clothes marked him out as a priest, but as we approached him, it was the expression on his face that really drew my attention. He was scowling at us, his face all twisted up. And then, dramatically, he made a huge sign of the cross, actually standing on tiptoe as he began it, stretching the forefinger of his right hand as high into the sky as he could. I'd seen priests make the sign before but never with such a big, exaggerated gesture, filled with so much anger. An anger that seemed directed toward us.

I supposed he'd some grievance against the Spook, or maybe against the work he did. I knew the trade made most people nervous, but I'd never seen a reaction like that.

"What was wrong with him?" I asked when we had passed him and were safely out of earshot.

"Priests!" snapped the Spook, the anger sharp in his voice. "They know everything but see nothing! And that one's worse than most. That's my other brother."

I'd have liked to know more but had the sense not to question him further. It seemed to me that there was a lot to learn about the Spook and his past, but I had a feeling they were things he'd only tell me when he was good and ready.

So I just followed him south, carrying his heavy bag and thinking about what my mam had written in the letter. She was never one to boast or make wild statements. Mam only said what had to be said, so she'd meant every single word. Usually she just got on with things and did what was necessary. The Spook had told me there was nothing much could be done about ghasts, but Mam had once silenced the ghasts on Hangman's Hill.

Being a seventh son of a seventh son was nothing that special in this line of work—you needed that just to be taken on as the Spook's apprentice. But I knew there was something else that made me different.

I was my mam's son, too.

CHAPTER V
BOGGARTS AND WITCHES

W<small>E</small> were heading for what the Spook called his Winter House.

As we walked, the last of the morning clouds melted away and I suddenly realized that there was something different about the sun. Even in the County, the sun sometimes shines in winter, which is good because it usually means that at least it isn't raining; but there's a time in each new year when you suddenly notice its warmth for the first time. It's just like the return of an old friend.

The Spook must have been thinking almost exactly the same thoughts, because he suddenly halted in his tracks, looked at me sideways, and gave me one of his rare smiles. "This is the first day of spring, lad," he said, "so we'll go to Chipenden."

It seemed an odd thing to say. Did he always go to Chipenden on the first day of the spring, and if so, why? So I asked him.

"Summer quarters. We winter on the edge of Anglezarke Moor and spend the summer in Chipenden."

"I've never heard of Anglezarke. Where's that?" I asked.

"To the far south of the County, lad. It's the place where I was born. We lived there until my father moved us to Horshaw."

Still, at least I'd heard of Chipenden, so that made me feel better. It struck me that, as the Spook's apprentice,

I'd be doing a lot of traveling and would have to learn how to find my way about.

Without further delay we changed direction, heading northeast toward the distant hills. I didn't ask any more questions, but that night, as we sheltered in a cold barn once more and supper was just a few more bites of the yellow cheese, my stomach began to think that my throat had been cut. I'd never been so hungry.

I wondered where we'd be staying in Chipenden and if we'd get something proper to eat there. I didn't know anyone who'd ever been there, but it was supposed to be a remote, unfriendly place somewhere up in the fells — the distant gray-and-purple hills that were just visible from my dad's farm. They always looked to me like huge sleeping beasts, but that was probably the fault of one of my uncles, who used to tell me tales like that. At night, he said, they started to move, and by dawn whole villages had sometimes disappeared from the face of the earth, crushed into dust beneath their weight.

❂ ❂ ❂

The next morning, dark gray clouds were covering the sun once more, and it looked as if we'd wait some time to see the second day of spring. The wind was getting up as well, tugging at our clothes as we gradually began to climb and hurling birds all over the sky, the clouds racing one another east to hide the summits of the fells.

Our pace was slow, and I was grateful for that because I'd developed a bad blister on each heel. So it was late in the day when we approached Chipenden, the light already beginning to fail.

By then, although it was still very windy, the sky had cleared and the purple fells were sharp against the skyline. The Spook hadn't talked much on the journey, but now he sounded almost excited as he called out the names of the fells one by one. There were names such as Parlick Pike, which was the nearest to Chipenden; others — some visible, some hidden and distant — were called Mellor Knoll, Saddle Fell, and Wolf Fell.

When I asked my master if there were any wolves on Wolf Fell, he smiled grimly. "Things change rapidly here, lad," he said, "and we must always be on our guard."

As the first rooftops of the village came into sight, the Spook pointed to a narrow path that led away from the road to twist upward by the side of a small, gurgling stream.

"My house is this way," he said. "It's a slightly longer route, but it means we can avoid going through the village. I like to keep my distance from the folk who live there. They prefer it that way, too."

I remembered what Jack had said about the Spook, and my heart sank. He'd been right. It was a lonely life. You ended up working by yourself.

There were a few stunted trees on each bank, clinging to the hillside against the force of the wind, but then suddenly, directly ahead was a wood of sycamore and ash; as we entered, the wind died away to a distant sigh. It was just a large collection of trees, a few hundred or so maybe, that offered shelter from the buffeting wind, but after a few moments I realized it was more than that.

I'd noticed before, from time to time, how some trees are noisy, always creaking their branches or rustling their leaves, while others hardly make any sound at all. Far above, I could hear the distant breath of the wind, but within the wood the only sounds to be heard were our boots. Everything was very still, a whole wood full of trees that were so silent it made a shiver run up and down my spine. It almost made me think that they were listening to us.

Then we came out into a clearing, and directly ahead was a house. It was surrounded by a tall hawthorn hedge so that just its upper story and the roof were visible. From the chimney rose a line of white smoke. Straight up into the air it went, undisturbed until, just above the trees, the wind chased it away to the east.

The house and garden, I noticed then, were sitting in a hollow in the hillside. It was just as if an obliging giant had come along and scooped away the ground with his hand.

I followed the Spook along the hedge until we reached a metal gate. The gate was small, no taller than my waist, and it had been painted a bright green, a job that had been completed so recently that I wondered if the paint had dried properly and whether the Spook would get it on his hand, which was already reaching toward the latch.

Suddenly something happened that made me catch my breath. Before the Spook touched the latch, it lifted up on its own and the gate swung slowly open as if moved by an invisible hand.

"Thank you," I heard the Spook say.

The front door didn't move by itself, because first it had to be unlocked with the large key that the Spook pulled from his pocket. It looked similar to the one he'd used to unlock the door of the house in Watery Lane.

"Is that the same key you used in Horshaw?" I asked.

"Aye, lad," he said, glancing down at me as he pushed open the door. "My brother, the locksmith, gave me this. It opens most locks as long as they're not too complicated. Comes in quite useful in our line of work."

The door yielded with a loud creak and a deep groan, and I followed the Spook into a small, gloomy hallway. There was a steep staircase to the right and a narrow flagged passage on the left.

"Leave everything at the foot of the stairs," said the

Spook. "Come on, lad. Don't dawdle. There's no time to waste. I like my food piping hot!"

So leaving his bag and my bundle where he'd said, I followed him down the passage toward the kitchen and the appetizing smell of hot food.

When we got there I wasn't disappointed. It reminded me of my mam's kitchen. Herbs were growing in big pots on the wide window ledge, and the setting sun was dappling the room with leaf-shadows. In the far corner a huge fire was blazing, filling the room with warmth, and right in the middle of the flagged floor was a large oaken table. On it were two enormous empty plates and, at its center, five serving dishes piled high with food next to a jug filled to the brim with hot, steaming gravy.

"Sit down and tuck in, lad," invited the Spook, and I didn't need to be asked twice.

I helped myself to large slices of chicken and beef, hardly leaving enough room on my plate for the mound of roasted potatoes and vegetables that followed. Finally

I topped it off with a gravy so tasty that only my mam could have done better.

I wondered where the cook was and how she'd known we'd be arriving just at that exact time to put out the hot food ready on the table. I was full of questions, but I was also tired, so I saved all my energy for eating. When I'd finally swallowed my last mouthful, the Spook had already cleared his own plate.

"Enjoy that?" he asked.

I nodded, almost too full to speak. I felt sleepy.

"After a diet of cheese, it's always good to come home to a hot meal," he said. "We eat well here. It makes up for the times when we're working."

I nodded again and started to yawn.

"There's lots to do tomorrow, so get yourself off to bed. Yours is the room with the green door, at the top of the first flight of stairs," the Spook told me. "Sleep well, but stay in your room and don't go wandering about during the night. You'll hear a bell ring when breakfast's ready. Go down as soon as you hear it—when someone's cooked good food he may get angry if you let it go cold. But don't come down too early either, because that could be just as bad."

I nodded, thanked him for the meal, and went down the passage toward the front of the house. The Spook's bag and my bundle had disappeared. Wondering who could have moved them, I climbed the stairs to bed.

My new room turned out to be much larger than my bedroom at home, which at one time I'd had to share with two of my brothers. This new room had space for a bed, a small table with a candle, a chair, and a dresser, but there was still lots of room to walk about in as well. And there, on top of the dresser, my bundle of belongings was waiting.

Directly opposite the door was a large sash window, divided into eight panes of glass so thick and uneven that I couldn't see much but whorls and swirls of color from outside. The window didn't look as if it had been opened for years. The bed was pushed right up along the wall beneath it, so I pulled off my boots, kneeled up on the quilt, and tried to open the window. Although it was a bit stiff, it proved easier than it had looked. I used the sash cord to raise the bottom half of the window in a series of jerks, just far enough to pop my head out and have a better look around.

I could see a wide lawn below me, divided into two by a path of white pebbles that disappeared into the trees. Above the tree line to the right were the fells, the nearest one so close that I felt I could almost reach out and touch it. I sucked in a deep breath of cool fresh air and smelled the grass before pulling my head back inside and unwrapping my small bundle of belongings. They fitted easily into the dresser's top drawer. As I was closing it, I suddenly noticed the writing on the far wall, in the shadows opposite the foot of the bed.

It was covered in names, all scrawled in black ink on the bare plaster. Some names were larger than others, as if those who'd written them thought a lot of themselves. Many had faded with time, and I wondered if they were the names of other apprentices who'd slept in this very room. Should I add my own name or wait until the end of the first month, when I might be taken on permanently? I didn't have a pen or ink, so it was something to think about later, but I examined the wall more closely, trying to decide which was the most recent name.

I decided it was BILLY BRADLEY—that seemed the clearest and had been squeezed into a small space as the wall filled up. For a few moments I wondered what Billy was doing now, but I was tired and ready for sleep.

The sheets were clean and the bed inviting, so, wasting no more time, I undressed, and the very moment my head touched the pillow I fell asleep.

When I next opened my eyes, the sun was streaming through the window. I'd been dreaming and had been woken suddenly by a noise. I thought it was probably the breakfast bell.

I felt worried then. Had it really been the bell downstairs summoning me to breakfast or a bell in my dream? How could I be sure? What was I supposed to do? It seemed that I'd be in trouble with the cook whether I went down early or late. So, deciding that I probably *had* heard the bell, I dressed and went downstairs right away.

On my way down I heard a clatter of pots and pans coming from the kitchen, but the moment I eased open the door, everything became deathly silent.

I made a mistake then. I should have gone straight back upstairs, because it was obvious that the breakfast wasn't ready. The plates had been cleared away from last night's supper, but the table was still bare and the fireplace was full of cold ashes. In fact, the kitchen was chilly and, worse than that, it seemed to be growing colder by the second.

My mistake was in taking a step toward the table. No sooner had I done that than I heard something make a sound right behind me. It was an angry sound. There was no doubt about that. It was a definite hiss of anger, and it was very close to my left ear. So close that I felt the breath of it.

The Spook had warned me not to come down early, and I suddenly felt that I was in real danger.

As soon as I had entertained that thought, something hit me very hard on the back of the head; I staggered toward the door, almost losing my balance and falling headlong.

I didn't need a second warning. I ran from the room and up the stairs. Then, halfway up, I froze. There was someone standing at the top. Someone tall and menacing, silhouetted against the light from the door of my room.

I halted, unsure which way to go until I was reassured by a familiar voice. It was the Spook.

It was the first time I'd seen him without his long black cloak. He was wearing a black tunic and gray breeches, and I could see that, although he was a tall man with broad shoulders, the rest of his body was thin, probably because some days all he got was a nibble of cheese. He was like the very best farm laborers when they get older. Some, of course, just get fatter, but the majority—like the ones my dad sometimes hires for the harvest now that most of my brothers have left home—are thin, with tough, wiry bodies. "Thinner means fitter," Dad always says, and now, looking at the Spook, I could see why he was able to walk at such a furious pace and for so long without resting.

"I warned you about going down early," he said quietly. "No doubt you got your ears boxed. Let that be a lesson to you, lad. Next time it might be far worse."

"I thought I heard the bell," I said. "But it must have been a bell in my dream."

The Spook laughed softly. "That's one of the first and most important lessons that an apprentice has to learn," he said; "the difference between waking and dreaming. Some never learn that."

He shook his head, took a step toward me, and patted me on the shoulder. "Come, I'll show you round the garden. We've got to start somewhere, and it'll pass the time until breakfast's ready."

When the Spook led me out, using the back door of the house, I saw that the garden was very large, much larger than it had looked from outside the hedge.

We walked east, squinting into the early morning sun, until we reached a wide lawn. The previous evening I'd thought that the garden was completely surrounded by the hedge, but now I realized that I was mistaken. There were gaps in it, and directly ahead was the wood. The path of white pebbles divided the lawn and vanished into the trees.

"There's really more than one garden," said the Spook. "Three, in fact, each reached by a path like this. We'll look at the eastern garden first. It's safe enough when the sun's up, but never walk down this path after dark. Well, not unless you have very good reason and certainly never when you're alone."

Nervously I followed the Spook toward the trees. The grass was longer at the edge of the lawn, and it was dotted with bluebells. I like bluebells because they flower in spring and always remind me that the long, hot days of summer are not too far away, but now I hardly gave them a second glance. The morning sun was hidden by the trees and the air had suddenly gotten much cooler. It reminded me of my visit to the kitchen. There was something strange and dangerous about this part of the woods, and it seemed to be getting steadily colder the farther we advanced into the trees.

There were rooks' nests high above us, and the birds' harsh, angry cries made me shiver even more than the cold. They were about as musical as my dad, who used to start singing as we got to the end of the milking. If the milk ever went sour, my mam used to blame it on him.

The Spook halted and pointed to the ground about five paces ahead. "What's that?" he asked, his voice hardly more than a whisper.

The grass had been cleared, and at the center of the large patch of bare earth was a gravestone. It was vertical but leaning slightly to the left. On the ground before it, six feet of soil was edged with smaller stones, which was unusual. But there was something else even more strange: across the top of the patch of earth, and fastened to the outer stones by bolts, lay thirteen thick iron bars.

I counted them twice just to be sure.

"Well, come on, lad—I asked you a question. What is it?"

My mouth was so dry I could hardly speak, but I managed to stammer out three words: "It's a grave. . . ."

"Good lad. Got it first time. Notice anything unusual?" he asked.

I couldn't speak at all by then. So I just nodded.

He smiled and patted me on the shoulder. "There's nothing to be afraid of. It's just a dead witch, and a pretty feeble one at that. They buried her on unhallowed ground outside a churchyard not too many miles from here. But she kept scratching her way to the surface. I gave her a good talking-to, but she wouldn't listen, so I had her brought here. It makes people feel better. That way they can get on with their lives in peace. They don't want to think about things like this. That's our job."

I nodded again and suddenly realized that I wasn't breathing, so I sucked in a deep lungful of air. My heart was hammering away in my chest, threatening to break out any minute, and I was trembling from head to foot.

"No, she's little trouble now," the Spook continued. "Sometimes, at the full moon, you can hear her stirring, but she lacks the strength to get to the surface and the iron bars would stop her anyway. But there are worse things farther off, there in the trees," he said, gesturing east with his bony finger. "About another twenty paces would bring you to the spot."

Worse? What could be worse? I wondered, but I knew he was going to tell me anyway.

"There are two other witches. One's dead and one's alive. The dead one's buried vertically, head down, but even then, once or twice each year we have to straighten out the bars over her grave. Just keep well away after dark."

"Why bury her head down?" I asked.

"That's a good question, lad," the Spook said. "You see, the spirit of a dead witch is usually what we call 'bone-bound.' They're trapped inside their bones, and some don't even know they're dead. We try them first head up and that's enough for most. All witches are different, but some are really stubborn. Still bound to her bones, a witch like that tries hard to get back into the world. It's as if they want to be born again, so we have to make things difficult for them and bury them the other way up. Coming out feet first isn't easy. Human babies sometimes have the same trouble. But she's still dangerous, so keep well away.

"Make sure you keep clear of the live one. She'd be

more dangerous dead than alive, because a witch that powerful would have no trouble at all getting back into the world. That's why we keep her in a pit. Her name's Mother Malkin, and she talks to herself. Well, it's more of a whisper really. She's just about as evil as you can get, but she's been in her pit for a long time and most of her power's bled away into the earth. She'd love to get her hands on a lad like you. So stay well away. Promise me now that you won't go near. Let me hear you say it."

"I promise not to go near," I whispered, feeling uneasy about the whole thing. It seemed a terrible, cruel thing to keep any living creature—even a witch—in the ground, and I couldn't imagine my mam liking the idea much.

"That's a good lad. We don't want any more accidents like the one this morning. There are worse things than getting your ears boxed. Far worse."

I believed him, but I didn't want to hear about it. Still, he had other things to show me, so I was spared more of his scary words. He led me out of the wood and strode toward another lawn.

"This is the southern garden," the Spook said. "Don't come here after dark either." The sun was quickly hidden by dense branches and the air grew steadily cooler, so I knew we were approaching something bad. He halted about ten paces short of a large stone that lay flat on the ground, close to the roots of an oak tree. It covered an area a bit larger than a grave, and judging by the part that was above ground, the stone was very thick, too.

"What do you think's buried under there?" the Spook asked.

I tried to appear confident. "Another witch?"

"No," said the Spook. "You don't need as much stone as that for a witch. Iron usually does the trick. But the thing under there could slip through iron bars in the twinkling of an eye. Look closely at the stone. Can you see what's carved on it?"

Gregory

I nodded. I recognized the letter, but I didn't know what it meant.

"That's the Greek letter beta," said the Spook. "It's the sign we use for a boggart. The diagonal line means it's been artificially bound under that stone and the name underneath tells you who did it. Bottom right is the Roman numeral for one. That means it's a boggart of the first rank and very dangerous. As I mentioned, we use grades from one to ten. Remember that—one day it might save your life. A grade ten is so weak that most folk wouldn't even notice it was there. A grade one could easily kill you. Cost me a fortune to have that stone brought here, but it was worth every penny. That's a bound boggart now. It's artificially bound and it'll stay there until Gabriel blows his horn.

"There's a lot you need to learn about boggarts, lad, and I'm going to start your training right after breakfast, but there is one important difference between those that are bound and those that are free. A free boggart can often travel miles from its home and, if it's so inclined, do endless mischief. If a boggart's particularly troublesome and won't listen to reason, then it's our job to bind it. Do it well and it's what we call artificially bound. Then it can't move at all. Of course, it's far easier said than done."

The Spook frowned suddenly, as if he'd remembered something unpleasant. "One of my apprentices got into serious trouble trying to bind a boggart," he said, shaking his head sadly, "but as it's only your first day, we won't talk about that yet."

Just then, from the direction of the house, the sound of a bell could be heard in the distance. The Spook smiled. "Are we awake or are we dreaming?" he asked.

"Awake."

"Are you sure?"

I nodded.

"In that case, let's go and eat," he said. "I'll show you the other garden when our bellies are full."

CHAPTER VI
A Girl with Pointy Shoes

THE kitchen had changed since my last visit. A small fire had been made up in the grate and two plates of bacon and eggs were on the table. There was a freshly baked loaf, too, and a large pat of butter.

"Tuck in, lad, before it gets cold," invited the Spook.

I set to immediately, and it didn't

take us long to finish off both platefuls and eat half the loaf as well. Then the Spook leaned back in his chair, tugged at his beard, and asked me an important question.

"Don't you think," he asked, his eyes staring straight into mine, "that was the best plate of bacon and eggs you've ever tasted?"

I didn't agree. The breakfast had been well cooked. It was good, all right, better than cheese, but I'd tasted better. I'd tasted better every single morning when I'd lived at home. My mam was a far better cook, but somehow I didn't think that was the answer the Spook was looking for. So I told a little white lie, the kind of untruth that doesn't really do any harm and tends to make people happier for hearing it.

"Yes," I said, "it was the very best breakfast that I've ever tasted. And I'm sorry for coming down too early and I promise that it won't happen again."

At that, the Spook grinned so much that I thought his face was going to split in two; then he clapped me on the back and led me out into the garden again.

It was only when we were outside that the grin finally faded. "Well done, lad," he said. "There are two things that respond well to flattery: boggarts and some women. Gets them every time."

Well, I hadn't seen any sign of a woman in the kitchen, so it confirmed what I'd suspected—that a boggart cooked our meals. It was a surprise, to say the least. Everyone thought that a spook was a boggart-slayer, or that he fixed them so they couldn't get up to any mischief. Who would have credited that he had one cooking and cleaning for him?

"This is the western garden," the Spook told me as we walked along the third path, the white pebbles crunching under our feet. "It's a safe place to be whether it's day or night. I often come here myself when I've got a problem that needs thinking through."

We passed through another gap in the hedge and were soon walking through the trees. I felt the difference right away. The birds were singing, and the trees were swaying slightly in the morning breeze. It was a happier place.

We kept walking until we came out of the trees onto a

hillside with a view of the fells to our right. The sky was so clear that I could see the dry-stone walls that divided the lower slopes into fields and marked out each farmer's territory. In fact, the view extended right to the summits of the nearest fell.

The Spook gestured toward a wooden bench to our left. "Take a pew, lad," he invited.

I did as I was told and sat down. For a few moments the Spook stared down at me, his green eyes locked upon mine. Then he began to pace up and down in front of the bench without speaking. He was no longer looking at me but stared into space with a vacant expression in his eyes. He thrust back his long black cloak and put his hands in his breeches pockets. Then, very suddenly, he sat down beside me and asked questions.

"How many different types of boggart do you think there are?"

I hadn't a clue. "I know two types already," I said, "the free and the bound. But I couldn't even begin to guess about the others."

"That's good twice over, lad. You've remembered what I taught you and you've shown yourself to be someone who doesn't make wild guesses. You see, there are as many different types of boggart as there are types of people, and each one has a personality of its own. Having said that, though, there are some types that can be recognized and given a name—sometimes on account of the shape they take and sometimes because of their behavior and the tricks they get up to."

He reached into his right pocket and pulled out a small book bound with black leather. Then he handed it to me. "Here, this is yours now," he said. "Take care of it, and whatever you do, don't lose it."

The smell of leather was very strong and the book appeared to be brand new. It was a bit of a disappointment to open it and find it full of blank pages. I suppose I'd expected it to be full of the secrets of the Spook's trade—but no, it seemed that I was expected to write them down, because next the Spook pulled a pen and a small bottle of ink from his pocket.

"Prepare to take notes," he said, standing up and beginning to pace back and forth in front of the bench again. "And be careful not to spill the ink, lad. It doesn't dribble from a cow's udder."

I managed to uncork the bottle. Then, very carefully, I dipped the nib of the pen into it and opened the notebook at the first page.

The Spook had already begun the lesson, and he was talking very fast.

"Firstly, there are hairy boggarts, which take the shape of animals. Most are dogs, but there are almost as many cats and the odd goat or two. But don't forget to include horses as well—they can be very tricky. And whatever their shape, hairy boggarts can be divided up into those that are hostile, friendly, or somewhere between.

"Then there are hall knockers, which sometimes develop into stone chuckers, which can get very angry when provoked. One of the nastiest types of all is the cattle ripper, because it's just as partial to human blood. But don't run away with the idea that we spooks just deal with boggarts, because the unquiet dead are never very far away. Then, to make things worse, witches are a real problem in the County. We don't have any local witches to worry about now, but to the east, near Pendle Hill, they're a real menace. And remember, not all witches are the same. They fall into four rough categories—the malevolent, the benign, the falsely accused, and the unaware."

By now, as you might have guessed, I was in real trouble. To begin with, he was talking so fast I hadn't managed to write down a single word. Secondly, I didn't even know all the big words he was using. However, just then he paused. I think he must have noticed the dazed expression on my face.

"What's the problem, lad?" he asked. "Come on, spit it out. Don't be afraid to ask questions."

"I didn't understand all that you said about witches," I said. "I don't know what 'malevolent' means. Or 'benign' either."

"Malevolent means evil," he explained. "Benign means good. And an unaware witch means a witch who doesn't know she's a witch, and because she's a woman that makes her double trouble. Never trust a woman."

"My mother's a woman," I said, suddenly feeling a little angry, "and I trust her."

"Mothers usually are women," said the Spook. "And mothers are usually quite trustworthy, as long as you're their son. Otherwise, look out! I had a mother once and I trusted her, so I remember the feeling well.

"Do you like girls?" he asked suddenly.

"I don't really know any girls," I admitted. "I don't have any sisters."

"Well, in that case you could fall easy victim to their tricks. So watch out for the village girls. Especially any who wear pointy shoes. Jot that down. It's as good a place to start as any."

I wondered what was so terrible about wearing pointy shoes. I knew my mam wouldn't be happy with what the Spook had just said. She believed you should take people as you find them, not just depend on someone else's opinion. Still, what choice did I have? So at the top of the very first page I wrote down *Village Girls with Pointy Shoes*.

He watched me write, then asked for the book and pen. "Look," he said, "you're going to have to take notes faster than that. There's a lot to learn, and you'll have filled a dozen notebooks before long, but for now three or four headings will be enough to get you started."

He then wrote *Hairy Boggarts* at the top of page two. Then *Hall Knockers* at the top of page three; then, finally, *Witches* at the top of page four.

"There," he said. "That's got you started. Just write anything you learn today under one of those four headings. But now for something more urgent. We need provisions. So go down to the village, or we'll go hungry tomorrow. Even the best cook can't cook without provisions. Remember that everything goes inside my sack. The butcher has it, so go there first. Just ask for Mr. Gregory's order.'

He gave me a small silver coin, warning me not to lose my change, then sent me off down the hill on the quickest route to the village.

Soon I was walking through trees again, until at last

I reached a stile that brought me onto a steep, narrow lane. A hundred or so paces lower, I turned a corner and the gray slates of Chipenden's rooftops came into view.

The village was larger than I'd expected. There were at least a hundred cottages, then a pub, a schoolhouse, and a big church with a bell tower. There was no sign of a market square, but the cobbled main street, which sloped quite steeply, was full of women with loaded baskets scurrying in and out of shops. Horses and carts were waiting on both sides of the street, so it was clear that the local farmers' wives came here to shop and, no doubt, also folk from hamlets nearby.

I found the butcher's shop without any trouble and joined a queue of boisterous women, all calling out to the butcher, a cheerful, big, red-faced man with a ginger beard. He seemed to know every single one of them by name, and they kept laughing loudly at his jokes, which came thick and fast. I didn't understand most of them, but the women certainly did, and they really seemed to be enjoying themselves.

Nobody paid me much attention, but at last I reached the counter and it was my turn to be served.

"I've called for Mr. Gregory's order," I told the butcher.

As soon as I'd spoken, the shop became quiet and the laughter stopped. The butcher reached behind the counter and pulled out a large sack. I could hear people whispering behind me, but even straining my ears, I couldn't quite catch what they were saying. When I glanced behind, they were looking everywhere but at me. Some were even staring down at the floor.

I gave the butcher the silver coin, checked my change carefully, thanked him, and carried the sack out of the shop, swinging it up onto my shoulder when I reached the street. The visit to the greengrocer's took no time at all. The provisions there were already wrapped, so I put the parcel in the sack, which was now starting to feel a bit heavy.

Until then everything had gone well, but as I went into the baker's, I saw the gang of lads.

There were seven or eight of them sitting on a garden wall. Nothing odd about that, except for the fact that they weren't speaking to one another—they were all busy staring at me with hungry faces, like a pack of wolves, watching every step I took as I approached the baker's.

When I came out of the shop they were still there, and now, as I began to climb the hill, they started to follow me. Well, although it was too much of a coincidence to think that they'd just decided to go up the same hill, I wasn't that worried. Six brothers had given me plenty of practice at fighting.

I heard the sound of their boots getting closer and closer. They were catching up with me pretty quickly, but maybe that was because I was walking slower and slower. You see, I didn't want them to think I was scared, and in any case, the sack was heavy and the hill I was climbing was very steep.

They caught up with me about a dozen paces before the stile, just at the point where the lane divided a small wood, the trees crowding in on either side to shut out the morning sun.

"Open the sack and let's see what we've got," said a voice behind me.

It was a loud, deep voice accustomed to telling people what to do. There was a hard edge of danger that told me its owner liked to cause pain and was always looking for his next victim.

I turned to face him but gripped the sack even tighter, keeping it firmly on my shoulder. The one who'd spoken was the leader of the gang. There was no doubt about that. The rest of them had thin, pinched faces, as if they were in need of a good meal, but he looked as if he'd been eating for all of them. He was at least a head taller than me, with broad shoulders and a neck like a bull's. His face was broad, too, with red cheeks, but his eyes were very small and he didn't seem to blink at all.

I suppose if he hadn't been there and hadn't tried to bully me, I might have relented. After all, some of the boys looked half starved, and there were a lot of apples and cakes in the sack. On the other hand, they weren't mine to give away.

"This doesn't belong to me," I said. "It belongs to Mr. Gregory."

"His last apprentice didn't let that bother him," said the leader, moving his big face closer to mine. "He used to open the sack for us. If you've any sense, you'll do the same. If you won't do it the easy way, then it'll have to be the hard way. But you won't like that very much and it'll all come down to the same thing in the end."

The gang began to move in closer, and I could feel someone behind me tugging at the sack. Even then, I wouldn't let go, and I stared back into the piggy eyes of the leader, trying hard not to blink.

At that moment something happened that took us all by surprise. There was a movement in the trees somewhere to my right, and we all turned toward it.

There was a dark shape in the shadows, and as my eyes adjusted to the gloom, I saw that it was a girl. She was moving slowly in our direction, but her approach was so silent that you could have heard a pin drop, and so smooth that she seemed to be floating rather than walking. Then she stopped just on the edge of the tree shadows, as if she didn't want to step into the sunlight.

"Why don't you leave him be?" she demanded. It seemed like a question but the tone in her voice told me it was a command.

"What's it to you?" asked the leader of the gang, jutting his chin forward and bunching his fists.

"Ain't me you need to worry about," she answered from the shadows. "Lizzie's back, and if you don't do what I say, it's her you'll answer to."

"Lizzie?" asked the lad, taking a step backward.

"Bony Lizzie. She's my aunt. Don't tell me you ain't heard of her. . . ."

Have you ever felt time slow so much that it almost appears to stop? Ever listened to a clock when the next tick seems to take forever to follow the last tock? Well, it was just like that until, very suddenly, the girl hissed loudly through her clenched teeth. Then she spoke again.

"Go on," she said. "Be off with you! Be gone, be quick or be dead!"

The effect on the gang was immediate. I glimpsed the expression on some of their faces and saw that they weren't just afraid. They were terrified and close to panic. Their leader turned on his heels and immediately fled down the hill, with the others close behind him.

I didn't know why they were so scared, but I felt like running, too. The girl was staring at me with wide eyes, and I didn't feel able to control my limbs properly. I felt like a mouse paralyzed by the stare of a stoat about to pounce at any moment.

I forced my left foot to move and slowly turned my body toward the trees to follow the direction my nose was pointing, but I was still gripping the Spook's sack. Whoever she was, I still wasn't going to give it up.

"Ain't you going to run as well?" she asked me.

I shook my head, but my mouth was very dry and I couldn't trust myself to try and speak. I knew the words would come out wrong.

She was probably about my own age—if anything, slightly younger. Her face was nice enough, for she had large brown eyes, high cheekbones, and long black hair. She wore a black dress tied tightly at the waist with a piece of white string. But as I took all this in, I suddenly noticed something that troubled me.

The girl was wearing pointy shoes, and immediately I remembered the Spook's warning. But I stood my ground, determined not to run like the others.

"Ain't you going to thank me?" she asked. "Be nice to get some thanks."

"Thanks," I said lamely, just managing to get the word out first time.

"Well, that's a start," she said. "But to thank me properly, you need to give me something, don't you? A cake and an apple will do for now. It ain't much to ask. There's plenty in the sack and Old Gregory won't notice, and if he does, he won't say anything."

I was shocked to hear her call the Spook "Old Gregory." I knew he wouldn't like being called that, and it told me two things. First, the girl had little respect for him, and second, she wasn't the least bit afraid of him. Back where

I came from, most people shivered even at the thought that the Spook might be in the neighborhood.

"I'm sorry," I said, "but I can't do that. They're not mine to give."

She glared at me hard then and didn't speak for a long time. I thought at one point that she was going to hiss at me through her teeth. I stared back at her, trying not to blink, until at last a faint smile lit up her face and she spoke again.

"Then I'll have to settle for a promise."

"A promise?" I asked, wondering what she meant.

"A promise to help me just as I helped you. I don't need any help right now, but perhaps one day I might."

"That's fine," I told her. "If you ever need any help in the future, then just ask."

"What's your name?" she asked, giving me a really broad smile.

"Tom Ward."

"Well, my name's Alice and I live yonder," she said, pointing back through the trees. "I'm Bony Lizzie's favorite niece."

Bony Lizzie was a strange name, but it would have been rude to mention it. Whoever she was, her name had been enough to scare the village lads.

That was the end of our conversation. We both turned then to go our separate ways, but as we walked away, Alice called over her shoulder, "Take care now. You don't want to end up like Old Gregory's last apprentice."

"What happened to him?" I asked.

"Better ask Old Gregory!" she shouted as she disappeared back into the trees.

When I got back, the Spook checked the contents of the sack carefully, ticking things off from a list.

"Did you have any trouble down in the village?" he asked when he'd finally finished.

"Some lads followed me up the hill and asked me to open the sack, but I told them no," I said.

"That was very brave of you," said the Spook. "Next time it won't do any harm to let them have a few apples and cakes. Life's hard enough as it is, but some of them come from very poor families. I always order extra in case they ask for some."

I felt annoyed then. If only he'd told me that in advance! "I didn't like to do it without asking you first," I said.

The Spook raised his eyebrows. "Did you want to give them a few apples and cakes?"

"I don't like being bullied," I said, "but some of them did look really hungry."

"Then next time trust your instincts and use your initiative," said the Spook. "Trust the voice inside you. It's rarely wrong. A spook depends a lot on that because it can sometimes mean the difference between life and death. So that's another thing we need to find out about you. Whether or not your instincts can be relied on."

He paused, staring at me hard, his green eyes searching my face. "Any trouble with girls?" he asked suddenly.

It was because I was still annoyed that I didn't give a straight answer to his question.

"No trouble at all," I answered.

It wasn't a lie because Alice had helped me, which was

the opposite of trouble. Still, I knew he really meant had I met any girls, and I knew I should have told him about her. Especially with her wearing pointy shoes.

I made lots of mistakes as an apprentice, and that was my second serious one—not telling the Spook the whole truth.

The first, even more serious one was making the promise to Alice.

CHAPTER VII
SOMEONE HAS TO DO IT

After that my life settled into a busy routine. The Spook taught me fast and made me write until my wrist ached and my eyes stung.

One afternoon he took me to the far end of the village, beyond the last stone cottage to a small circle of willow trees, which are called withy trees in the County. It was a gloomy spot and there, hanging from a branch, was a rope. I looked up and saw a big brass bell.

"When people need help," said the Spook, "they don't come up to the house. Nobody comes unless they're invited. I'm strict about that. They come down here and ring that bell. Then we go to them."

The trouble was that even after weeks had gone by, nobody came to ring the bell, and I only ever got to go farther than the western garden when it was time to fetch the weekly provisions from the village. I was lonely, too, missing my family, so it was a good job the Spook kept me busy—that meant I didn't have time to dwell on it. I always went to bed tired and fell asleep as soon as my head hit the pillow.

The lessons were the most interesting part of each day, but I didn't learn much about ghasts, ghosts, and witches. The Spook had told me that the main topic in an apprentice's first year was boggarts, together with such subjects as botany, which meant learning all about plants, some of which were really useful as medicines or could be eaten if you had no other food. But my lessons weren't just writing. Some of the work was just as hard and physical as anything I'd done back home on our farm.

It started on a warm, sunny morning, when the Spook told me to put away my notebook and led the way toward his southern garden. He gave me two things to carry: a spade and a long measuring rod.

"Free boggarts travel down leys," he explained. "But sometimes something goes wrong. It can be the result of a storm or maybe even an earthquake. In the County there hasn't been a serious earthquake in living memory, but that doesn't matter, because leys are all interconnected and something happening to one, even a thousand miles away, can disturb all the others. Then boggarts get stuck in the same place for years, and we call them 'naturally bound.' Often they can't move more than a few dozen paces in any direction, and they cause little trouble. Not unless you happen to get too close to one. Sometimes, though, they can be stuck in awkward places, close to a house or even inside one. Then you might need to move the boggart from there and artificially bind it elsewhere."

"What's a ley?" I asked.

"Not everybody agrees, lad," he told me. "Some think they're just ancient paths that crisscross the land, the paths our forefathers walked in ancient times when men were real men and darkness knew its place. Health was better, lives were longer, and everyone was happy and content."

"What happened?"

"Ice moved down from the north and the earth grew cold for thousands of years," the Spook explained. "It was so difficult to survive that men forgot everything they'd learned. The old knowledge was unimportant. Keeping warm and eating was all that mattered. When the ice finally pulled back, the survivors were hunters dressed in animal skins. They'd forgotten how to grow crops and husband animals. Darkness was all-powerful.

"Well, it's better now, although we still have a long way to go. All that's left of those times are the leys, but the truth is they're more than just paths. Leys are really lines of power far beneath the earth. Secret invisible roads that free boggarts can use to travel at great speed. It's these free boggarts that cause the most trouble. When they set up home in a new location, often they're not welcome. Not being welcome makes them angry. They play tricks—sometimes dangerous tricks—and that means work for us. Then they need to be artificially bound in a pit. Just like the one that you're going to dig now. . . .

"This is a good place," he said, pointing at the ground near a big, ancient oak tree. "I think there should be enough space between the roots."

The Spook gave me a measuring rod so that I could make the pit exactly six feet long, six feet deep, and three feet wide. Even in the shade it was too warm to be digging, and it took me hours and hours to get it right because the Spook was a perfectionist.

After digging the pit, I had to prepare a smelly mixture of salt, iron filings, and a special sort of glue made from bones.

"Salt can burn a boggart," said the Spook. "Iron, on

the other hand, earths things: Just as lightning finds its way to earth and loses its power, iron can sometimes bleed away the strength and substance of things that haunt the dark. It can end the mischief of troublesome boggarts. Used together, salt and iron form a barrier that a boggart can't cross. In fact, salt and iron can be useful in lots of situations."

After stirring up the mixture in a big metal bucket, I used a large brush to line the inside of the pit. It was like painting but harder work, and the coating had to be perfect in order to stop even the craftiest boggart from escaping.

"Do a thorough job, lad," the Spook told me. "A boggart can escape through a hole no bigger than a pinhead."

Of course, as soon as the pit was completed to the Spook's satisfaction, I had to fill it in and begin again. He had me digging two practice pits a week, which was hard, sweaty work and took up a lot of my time. It was a bit scary, too, because I was working near pits that contained real boggarts, and even in daylight it was a creepy place. I noticed that the Spook never went too far away, though, and he always seemed watchful and alert, telling me you could never take chances with boggarts even when they were bound.

The Spook also told me that I'd need to know every inch of the County—all its towns and villages and the quickest route between any two points. The trouble was that although the Spook said he had lots of maps upstairs in his library, it seemed I always had to do things the hard way, so he started me off by making me draw a map of my own.

At its center was his house and gardens and it had to include the village and the nearest of the fells. The idea was that it would gradually get bigger to include more and more of the surrounding countryside. But drawing wasn't my strong point, and as I said, the Spook was a perfectionist, so the map took a long time to grow. It was only then that he started to show me his own maps, but he made me spend more time carefully folding them up afterward than actually studying them.

I also began to keep a diary. The Spook gave me another

notebook for this, telling me for the umpteenth time that I needed to record the past so that I could learn from it. I didn't write in it every day, though; sometimes I was too tired and sometimes my wrist was aching too much from scribbling at top speed in my other notebook while trying to keep up with what the Spook said.

Then, one morning at breakfast, when I'd been staying with the Spook for just one month, he asked, "What do you think so far, lad?"

I wondered if he were talking about the breakfast. Perhaps there'd be a second course to make up for the bacon, which had been a bit burned that morning. So I just shrugged. I didn't want to offend the boggart, which was probably listening.

"Well, it's a hard job and I wouldn't blame you for deciding to give it up now," he said. "After the first month's passed, I always give each new apprentice the chance to go home and think very carefully about whether he wants to carry on or not. Would you like to do the same?"

I did my best not to seem too eager, but I couldn't keep the smile off my face. The trouble was, the more I smiled the more miserable the Spook looked. I got the feeling that he wanted me to stay, but I couldn't wait to be off. The thought of seeing my family again and getting to taste Mam's cooking seemed like a dream.

I left for home within the hour. "You're a brave lad and your wits are sharp," he said to me at the gate. "You've passed your month's trial, so you can tell your dad that, if you want to carry on, I'll be visiting him in the autumn to collect my ten guineas. You've the makings of a good apprentice, but it's up to you, lad. If you don't come back, then I'll know you've decided against it. Otherwise I'll expect you back within the week. Then I'll give you five years' training that'll make you almost as good at the job as I am."

I set off for home with a light heart. You see, I didn't want to tell the Spook, but the moment he'd given me the chance to go home and maybe never come back, I'd already made up my mind to do just that. It was a terrible job.

From what the Spook had told me, apart from the loneliness, it was dangerous and terrifying. Nobody really cared whether you lived or died. They just wanted you to get rid of whatever was plaguing them but didn't think for a second about what it might cost you.

The Spook had described how he'd once been half killed by a boggart. It had changed, in the blink of an eye, from a hall knocker to a stone chucker and had nearly brained him with a rock as big as a blacksmith's fist. He said that he hadn't even been paid yet but expected to get the money next spring. Well, next spring was a long time off, so what good was that? As I set off for home, it seemed to me that I'd be better off working on the farm.

The trouble was, it was nearly two days' journey, and walking gave me a lot of time to think. I remembered how bored I'd sometimes been on the farm. Could I really put up with working there for the rest of my life?

Next I started to think about what Mam would say. She'd been really set on me being the Spook's apprentice, and if I stopped I'd really let her down. So the hardest part would be telling her and watching her reaction.

By nightfall on the first day of my journey home, I'd finished all the cheese the Spook had given me for the trip. So the next day I only stopped once, to bathe my feet in a stream, reaching home just before the evening milking.

As I opened the gate to the yard, Dad was heading for the cowshed. When he saw me, his face lit up with a broad smile. I offered to help with the milking so we could talk, but he told me to go in right away and speak to my mam.

"She's missed you, lad. You'll be a sight for sore eyes."

Patting me on the back, he went off to do his milking, but before I'd taken half a dozen paces Jack came out of the barn and made straight for me.

"What brings you back so soon?" he asked. He seemed a little bit cool. Well, to be honest, he was more cold than cool. His face was sort of twisted up, as if he were trying to scowl and grin at the same time.

"The Spook's sent me home for a few days. I've to make up my mind whether to carry on or not."

"So what will you do?"

"I'm going to talk to Mam about it."

"No doubt you'll get your own way, as usual," Jack said.

By now Jack was definitely scowling, and it made me feel that something had happened while I'd been away. Why else was he suddenly so unfriendly? Was it because he didn't want me coming home?

"And I can't believe you took Dad's tinderbox," he said.

"He gave it to me," I said. "He wanted me to have it."

"He offered it, but that didn't mean you had to take it. The trouble with you is that you only think about yourself. Think of poor Dad. He loved that tinderbox."

I didn't say anything because I didn't want to get into an argument. I knew he was wrong. Dad had wanted me to have the tinderbox, I was sure of it.

"While I'm back, I'll be able to help out," I said, trying to change the subject.

"If you really want to earn your keep, then feed the

pigs!" he called as he turned to walk away. It was a job neither of us liked much. They were big, hairy, smelly pigs and always so hungry that it was never safe to turn your back on them.

Despite what Jack had said, I was still glad to be home. As I crossed the yard, I glanced up at the house. Mam's climbing roses covered most of the wall at the back and always did well even though they faced north. Now they were just shooting, but by mid-June they'd be covered in red blossoms.

The back door was always jamming because the house had once been struck by lightning. The door had caught fire and had been replaced, but the frame was still slightly warped, so I had to push hard to force it open. It was worth it, because the first thing I saw was Mam's smiling face.

She was sitting in her old rocking chair in the far corner of the kitchen, a place where the setting sun couldn't reach. If the light was too bright, it hurt her eyes. Mam preferred winter to summer and night to day.

She was glad to see me all right, and at first I tried to delay telling her I'd come home to stay. I put on a brave face and pretended to be happy, but she saw right through me. I could never hide anything from her.

"What's wrong?" she asked.

I shrugged and tried to smile, probably doing even worse than my brother at disguising my feelings.

"Speak up," she said. "There's no point in keeping it bottled up."

I didn't answer for a long time because I was trying to find a way to put it into words. The rhythm of Mam's rocking chair gradually slowed, until at last it came to a complete halt. That was always a bad sign.

"I've passed my month's trial and Mr. Gregory says it's up to me whether I carry on or not. But I'm lonely, Mam," I confessed at last. "It's just as bad as I expected. I've got no friends. Nobody of my own age to talk to. I feel so alone—I'd like to come back and work here."

I could have said more and told her how happy we used to be on the farm when all my brothers were living at home. I didn't—I knew that she missed them, too. I thought she'd be sympathetic because of that, but I was wrong.

There was a long pause before Mam spoke, and I could hear Ellie sweeping up in the next room, singing softly to herself as she worked.

"Lonely?" Mam asked, her voice full of anger rather than sympathy. "How can you be lonely? You've got yourself, haven't you? If you ever lose yourself, then you'll really be lonely. In the meantime, stop complaining. You're nearly a man now, and a man has to work. Ever since the world began, men have been doing jobs they didn't like. Why should it be any different for you? You're the seventh son of a seventh son, and this is the job you were born to do."

"But Mr. Gregory's trained other apprentices," I blurted out. "One of them could come back and look after the County. Why does it have to be me?"

"He's trained many, but precious few completed their time," Mam said, "and those that did aren't a patch on him. They're flawed or weak or cowardly. They walk a twisted path, taking money for accomplishing little. So there's only you left now, son. You're the last chance. The last hope. Someone has to do it. Someone has to stand against the dark. And you're the only one who can."

The chair began to rock again, slowly picking up speed.

"Well, I'm glad that's settled. Do you want to wait for supper or shall I put you some out as soon as it's ready?" Mam asked.

"I've had nothing to eat all day, Mam. Not even breakfast."

"Well, it's rabbit stew. That ought to cheer you up a bit."

I sat at the kitchen table feeling as low and sad as I could ever remember while Mam bustled about the stove. The rabbit stew smelled delicious, and my mouth began to water. Nobody was a better cook than my mam, and it was worth coming home, even for just a single meal.

With a smile, Mam carried across a big steaming plate

of stew and set it down before me. "I'll go and make up your room," she said. "Now you're here, you might as well stay a couple of days."

I mumbled my thanks and wasted no time in starting. As soon as Mam went upstairs, Ellie came into the kitchen.

"Nice to see you back, Tom," she said with a smile. Then she looked down at my generous plate of food. "Would you like some bread with that?"

"Yes, please," I said, and Ellie buttered me three thick slices before sitting at the table opposite me. I finished it all without once coming up for air, finally wiping my plate clean with the last big slice of freshly baked bread.

"Feel better now?"

I nodded and tried to smile, but I knew it hadn't worked properly because Ellie suddenly looked worried. "I couldn't help overhearing what you told your mam," she said. "I'm sure it's not as bad as all that. It's just because the job's all new and strange. You'll soon get used to the work. Anyway, you don't have to go back right away.

After a few days at home you'll feel better. And you'll always be welcome here, even when the farm belongs to Jack."

"I don't think Jack's that pleased to see me."

"Why, what makes you say that?" Ellie asked.

"He just didn't seem that friendly, that's all. I don't think he wants me here."

"Don't you worry about your big mean brother. I can sort him out easily enough."

I smiled properly then, because it was true. As my mam once said, Ellie could twist Jack round her little finger.

"What's mainly bothering him is this," Ellie said, smoothing her hand down across her belly. "My mother's sister died in childbirth, and our family still talks of it to this day. It's made Jack nervous, but I'm not bothered at all, because I couldn't be in a better place, with your mam to look after me." She paused. "But there is something else. Your new job worries him."

"He seemed happy enough about it before I went away," I said.

"He was doing that for you because you're his brother and he cares about you. But the work a spook does frightens people. It makes them uneasy. I suppose if you'd left right away it would probably have been all right. But Jack said that on the day you left, you went straight up over the hill into the wood, and that since then the dogs have been uneasy. Now they won't even go into the north pasture.

"Jack thinks you've stirred something up. I suppose it all comes back to this," Ellie went on, patting her belly gently. "He's just being protective, that's all. He's thinking of his family. But don't worry. It'll all sort itself out eventually."

In the end I stayed three days, trying to put on a brave face, but eventually I sensed it was time to go. Mam was the last person I saw before I left. We were alone in the kitchen, and she gave my arm a squeeze and told me that she was proud of me.

"You're more than just seven times seven," she said,

smiling at me warmly. "You're my son, too, and you have the strength to do what has to be done."

I nodded in agreement because I wanted her to be happy, but the smile slipped from my face just as soon as I left the yard. I trudged back to the Spook's house with my heart right down in my boots, feeling hurt and disappointed that Mam wouldn't have me back home.

It rained all the way back to Chipenden, and when I arrived, I was cold, wet, and miserable. But as I reached the front gate, to my surprise the latch lifted on its own and the gate swung open without me touching it. It was a sort of welcome, an encouragement to go in, something I'd thought was reserved only for the Spook. I suppose I should have been pleased by that, but I wasn't. It just felt creepy.

I knocked at the door three times before I finally noticed that the key was in the lock. As my knocking had brought no response, I turned the key, then eased the door open.

I checked all the downstairs rooms but one. Then I called up the stairs. There was no answer, so I risked going into the kitchen.

There was a fire blazing in the grate and the table was set for one. At its center was a huge, steaming hot pot. I was so hungry I helped myself and had almost polished off the lot when I saw the note under the salt shaker.

Gone east to Pendle. It's witch trouble, so I'll be away for some time. Make yourself at home, but don't forget to pick up this week's provisions. As usual, the butcher has my sack, so go there first.

Pendle was a big fell, almost a mountain really, far to the east of the County. That whole district was infested with witches and was a risky place to go, especially alone. It reminded me again of how dangerous the Spook's job could be.

But at the same time I couldn't help feeling a bit annoyed. All that time waiting for something to happen, then the moment I'm away the Spook goes off without me!

◯ ◯ ◯

I slept well that night, but not so deeply that I failed to hear the bell summoning me to breakfast.

I went downstairs on time and was rewarded with the best plate of bacon and eggs I'd eaten in the Spook's house. I was so pleased that, just before leaving the table, I spoke out loud, using the words that my dad said every Sunday after lunch.

"That was really good," I said. "My compliments to the cook."

No sooner had I spoken than the fire flared up in the grate and a cat began to purr. I couldn't see a cat, but the noise it was making was so loud that I'll swear the windowpanes were rattling. It was obvious that I'd said the right thing.

So, feeling right pleased with myself, I set off for the village to pick up the provisions. The sun was shining out of a blue, cloudless sky, the birds were singing, and after the previous day's rain the whole world seemed bright and gleaming and new.

I started at the butcher's, collected the Spook's sack,

moved on to the greengrocer's, and finished at the baker's. Some village lads were leaning against the wall nearby. There weren't as many as last time, and their leader, the big lad with the neck like a bull's, wasn't with them.

Remembering what the Spook had said, I walked straight up to them. "I'm sorry about last time," I said, "but I'm new and didn't understand the rules properly. Mr. Gregory said that you can have an apple and a cake each." So saying, I opened the sack and handed each lad just what I'd promised. Their eyes opened so wide that they almost popped out of their sockets and each muttered his thanks.

At the top of the lane someone was waiting for me. It was the girl called Alice, and once again she was standing in the shadow of the trees as if she didn't like the sunlight.

"You can have an apple and a cake," I told her.

To my surprise she shook her head. "I'm not hungry at the moment," she said. "But there's something that I do want. I need you to keep your promise. I need some help."

I shrugged. A promise is a promise and I remembered making it. So what else could I do but keep my word?

"Tell me what you want and I'll do my best," I replied.

Once more her face lit up into a really broad smile. She wore a black dress and had pointy shoes, but that smile somehow made me forget all that. Still, what she said next set me worrying and quite spoiled the rest of the day.

"Ain't going to tell you now," she said. "Tell you this evening, I will, just as the sun goes down. Come to me when you hear Old Gregory's bell."

I heard the bell just before sunset, and with a heavy heart went down the hill toward the circle of willow trees where the lanes crossed. It didn't seem right, her ringing the bell like that. Not unless she had work for the Spook, but somehow I doubted that.

Far above, the last rays of the sun were bathing the

summits of the fells in a faint orange glow, but down below, among the withy trees, it was gray and full of shadows.

I shivered when I saw the girl, because she was pulling the rope with just one hand yet making the clappers of the big bell dance wildly. Despite her slim arms and narrow waist, she had to be very strong.

She stopped ringing as soon as I showed my face, and rested her hands on her hips while the branches continued to dance and shake overhead. We just stared at each other for ages, until my eyes were drawn down toward a basket at her feet. There was something inside it covered with a black cloth.

She lifted the basket and held it out to me.

"What is it?" I asked.

"It's for you, so that you can keep your promise."

I accepted it, but I wasn't feeling very happy. Curious, I reached inside to lift the black cloth.

"No, leave it be," Alice snapped, a sharp edge to her voice. "Don't let the air get to them or they'll spoil."

"What are they?" I asked. It was growing darker by

the minute, and I was starting to feel nervous.

"They're just cakes."

"Thank you very much," I said.

"They're not for you," she said, a little smile playing at the corners of her mouth. "Those cakes are for old Mother Malkin."

My mouth became dry, and a chill ran down my spine. Mother Malkin, the live witch the Spook kept in a pit in his garden.

"I don't think Mr. Gregory would like it," I said. "He told me to keep away from her."

"He's a very cruel man, Old Gregory," said Alice. "Poor Mother Malkin's been in that damp, dark hole in the ground for almost thirteen years now. Is it right to treat an old woman so badly?"

I shrugged. I hadn't been happy about it myself. It was hard to defend what he'd done, but he'd said there was a very good reason for it.

"Look," she said, "you won't get into trouble, because Old Gregory need never know. It's just comfort you're bringing to her. Her favorite cakes, made by family. Ain't nothing wrong with that. Just something to keep up her strength against the cold. Gets right into her bones, it does."

Once again I shrugged. All the best arguments seemed to belong to her.

"So just give her a cake each night. Three cakes for three nights. Best do it at midnight, because it's then that she gets most peckish. Give her the first one tonight."

Alice turned to go but stopped and turned to give me a smile. "We could become good friends, you and me," she said with a chuckle.

Then she disappeared into the deepening shadows.

CHAPTER VIII
OLD MOTHER MALKIN

Back at the Spook's cottage, I began to worry, but the more I thought about it, the less clear I was in my own mind. I knew what the Spook would say. He'd throw the cakes away and give me a long lesson on witches and problems with girls wearing pointy shoes.

He wasn't here, so that didn't enter

into it. There were two things that made me go into the darkness of the eastern garden, where he kept the witches. The first was my promise to Alice.

"Never make a promise that you're not prepared to keep," my dad always told me. So I had little choice. He'd taught me right from wrong, and just because I was the Spook's apprentice, it didn't mean I'd to change all my ways.

Second I didn't hold with keeping an old woman as a prisoner in a hole in the ground. Doing that to a dead witch seemed reasonable, but not to a live one. I remember wondering what terrible crime she'd committed to deserve that.

What harm could it do just to give her three cakes? A bit of comfort from her family against the cold and damp, that's all it was. The Spook had told me to trust my instincts, and after weighing things in the balance, I felt that I was doing the right thing.

The only problem was that I had to take the cakes myself, at midnight. It gets pretty dark by then, especially if there's no moon visible.

◉ ◉ ◉

I approached the eastern garden carrying the basket. It was dark, but not quite as dark as I'd expected. For one thing, my eyes have always been pretty sharp at night. My mam's good in the dark, and I think I get it from her side. And for another, it was a cloudless night and the moonlight helped me pick out my way.

As I entered the trees, it suddenly grew colder, and I shivered. By the time I reached the first grave, the one with the stone border and the thirteen bars, I felt even colder. That was where the first witch was buried. She was feeble, with little strength, or so the Spook had said. No need to worry there, I told myself, trying hard to believe it.

Making up my mind to give Mother Malkin the cakes in daylight was one thing, but now, down in the garden close to midnight, I was no longer so sure. The Spook had told me to keep well away after dark. He'd warned me more than once, so it had to be an important rule, and now I was breaking it.

There were all sorts of faint sounds. The rustlings and twitchings were probably nothing, just small creatures I'd disturbed moving out of my path, but they reminded me that I'd no right to be here.

The Spook had told me that the other two witches were about twenty paces farther on, so I counted out my steps carefully. That brought me to a second grave that was just like the first one. I got closer, just to be sure. There were the bars and you could see the earth just beneath them, hard-packed soil without even a single blade of grass. This witch was dead but was still dangerous. She was the one who had been buried head downward. That meant that the soles of her feet were somewhere just below the soil.

As I stared at the grave, I thought I saw something move. It was a sort of twitch; probably just my imagination, or maybe some small animal—a mouse or a shrew or something. I moved on quickly. What if it had been a toe?

Three more paces brought me to the place I was looking

for—there was no doubt about it. Again there was a border of stones with thirteen bars. There were three differences, though. First the area under the bars was a square rather than an oblong. Second, it was bigger, probably about four paces by four. Third, there was no packed earth under the bars, just a very black hole in the ground.

I halted in my tracks and listened carefully. There hadn't been much noise so far, just the faint rustlings of night creatures and a gentle breeze. A breeze so light that I'd hardly noticed it. I noticed it when it stopped, though. Suddenly everything was very still and the woods became unnaturally quiet.

You see, I had been listening to try and hear the witch, and now I sensed that she was listening to me.

The silence seemed to go on and on forever, until suddenly I became aware of a faint breathing from the pit. That sound somehow made it possible to move, so I took a few more steps till I was standing very close to its edge, with the toe of my boot actually touching the stone border.

At that moment I remembered something the Spook had told me about Mother Malkin. . . .

"Most of her power's bled away into the earth. She'd love to get her hands on a lad like you."

So I took a step backward—not too far, but the Spook's words had set me thinking. What if a hand came out of the pit and grabbed my ankle?

Wanting to get it over with, I called down gently into the darkness. "Mother Malkin," I said. "I've brought something for you. It's a present from your family. Are you there? Are you listening?"

There was no reply, but the rhythm of the breathing below seemed to quicken. So, wasting no more time and desperate to get back to the warmth of the Spook's house, I reached into the basket and felt under the cloth. My fingers closed upon one of the cakes. It felt sort of soft and squishy and a bit sticky. I pulled it out and held it over the bars.

"It's just a cake," I said softly. "I hope it makes you feel better. I'll bring you another one tomorrow night."

With those words, I let go of the cake and allowed it to fall into the darkness.

I should have gone back to the cottage immediately, but I stayed for a few more seconds to listen. I don't know what I expected to hear, but it was a mistake.

There was a movement in the pit, as if something were dragging itself along the ground. And then I heard the witch begin to eat the cake.

I thought some of my brothers made unpleasant noises at the table, but this was far worse. It sounded even more revolting than our big hairy pigs with their snouts in the swill bucket, a mixture of snuffling, snorting, and chewing mixed with heavy breathing. I didn't know whether or not she was enjoying the cake, but she certainly made enough noise about it.

That night I found it very hard to sleep. I kept thinking about the dark pit and worrying about having to visit it again the following night.

I only just made it down to breakfast on time, and the

bacon was burned and the bread a bit on the stale side. I couldn't understand why this was—I'd bought the bread fresh from the baker's only the day before. Not only that, the milk was sour. Could it be because the boggart was angry with me? Did it know what I'd been up to? Had it spoiled the breakfast as some sort of warning?

Working on a farm is hard, and that was what I was used to. The Spook hadn't left me any tasks to do, so I'd nothing to fill my day with. I did walk up to the library, thinking that he probably wouldn't mind if I found myself something useful to read, but to my disappointment the door was locked.

So what could I do but go for a walk? I decided to explore the fells, first climbing Parlick Pike; at the summit I sat on the cairn of stones and admired the view.

It was a clear, bright day and from up there I could see the County spread out below me, with the distant sea an inviting, twinkling blue, way out to the north-west. The fells seemed to go on forever, great hills with names like Calder Fell and Stake House Fell—so many that it seemed it would take a lifetime to explore them.

Nearby was Wolf Fell, and it made me wonder whether there actually were any wolves in the area. Wolves could be dangerous and it was said that in winter, when the weather was cold, they sometimes hunted in packs. Well, it was spring now, and I certainly didn't see any sign of them, but that didn't mean they weren't there. It made me realize that being up on the fells after nightfall would be quite scary.

Not as scary, I decided, as having to go and feed Mother Malkin another of the cakes, and all too soon the sun began to sink into the west and I was forced to climb down toward Chipenden again.

Once more I found myself carrying the basket through the darkness of the garden. This time I decided to get it over with quickly. Wasting no time, I dropped the second sticky cake through the bars into the black pit.

It was only when it was too late, the very second it left my fingers, that I noticed something that sent a chill straight to my heart.

The bars above the pit had been bent. Last night they'd been perfectly straight, thirteen parallel rods of iron. Now the center ones were almost wide enough to get a head through.

They could have been bent by someone on the outside, above ground, but I doubted that. The Spook had told me that the gardens and house were guarded and that nobody could get in. He hadn't said how and by what, but I guessed it was by some sort of boggart. Perhaps the same one that made the meals.

So it had to be the witch. She must have climbed up the side of the pit somehow and begun working at the bars. Suddenly the truth of what was happening dawned inside my head.

I'd been so stupid! The cakes were making her stronger.

I heard her below in the darkness, starting to eat the second cake, making the same horrible chewing, snuffling, and snorting noises. I left the trees quickly and went back to the cottage. For all I knew, she might not even need the third one.

○ ○ ○

After another sleepless night, I'd made up my mind. I decided to go and see Alice, give her back the last cake, and explain to her why I couldn't keep my promise.

First I had to find her. Straight after breakfast I went down to the wood where we'd first met and walked through to its far edge. Alice had said she lived "yonder," but there was no sign of any buildings, just low hills and valleys and more woods in the distance.

Thinking it would be faster to ask directions, I went down into the village. There were surprisingly few people about, but as I'd expected, some of the lads were hanging about near the baker's. It seemed to be their favorite spot. Perhaps they liked the smell. I know I did. Freshly baked bread has one of the best smells in all the world.

They weren't very friendly considering that last time we'd met, I'd given them a cake and an apple each. That was probably because this time the big lad with piggy eyes was with them. Still, they did listen to what I had to say. I didn't go into details—just told them I needed to find the girl we'd met at the edge of the wood.

"I know where she might be," said the big lad, scowling fiercely, "but you'd be stupid to go there."

"Why's that?"

"Didn't you hear what she said?" he asked, raising his eyebrows. "She said Bony Lizzie was her aunt."

"Who's Bony Lizzie?"

They looked at one another and shook their heads as if I was mad. Why was it that everyone seemed to have heard of her but me?

"Lizzie and her grandmother spent a whole winter here before Gregory sorted them out. My dad's always going on about them. They were just about the scariest witches there've ever been in these parts. They lived with something just as scary, though. It looked like a man but it was really big, with too many teeth to fit into its mouth. That's what my dad told me. He said that back then, during that long winter, people never went out after dark. Some spook you'll be if you've never even heard of Bony Lizzie."

I didn't like the sound of that one little bit. I realized

I'd been really stupid. If only I'd told the Spook about my talk with Alice, he'd have realized that Lizzie was back and would have done something about it.

According to the big lad's dad, Bony Lizzie had lived on a farm about three miles southeast of the Spook's place. It had been deserted for years, and nobody ever went there. So that was the most likely place she'd be staying now. That seemed about right to me, because it was in the direction that Alice had pointed.

Just then a group of grim-faced people came out of the church. They turned the corner in a straggly line and headed up the hill toward the fells, the village priest in the lead. They were dressed in warm clothing, and many of them were carrying walking sticks.

"What's all that about?" I asked.

"A child went missing last night," answered one of the lads, spitting onto the cobbles. "A three-year-old. They think he's wandered off up there. Mind you, it's not the first. Two days ago a baby went missing from a farm over on the Long Ridge. It was too young to walk, so it must have been carried off. They think it could be wolves. It was a bad winter, and that sometimes brings them back."

The directions I was given turned out to be pretty good. Even allowing for going back to pick up Alice's basket, it was less than an hour before Lizzie's house came into view.

At that point, in bright sunlight, I lifted the cloth and examined the last of the three cakes. It smelled bad but looked even worse. It seemed to have been made from small pieces of meat and bread, plus other things that I couldn't identify. It was wet and very sticky and almost black. None of the ingredients had been cooked but just sort of pressed together. Then I noticed something even more horrible. There were tiny white things crawling on the cake that looked like maggots.

I shuddered, covered it up with the cloth, and went down the hill to the very neglected farm. Fences were broken, the barn was missing half its roof, and there was no sign of any animals.

One thing *did* worry me, though. Smoke was coming from the farmhouse chimney. It meant that someone was at home, and I began to worry about the thing with too many teeth to fit into its mouth.

What had I expected? It was going to be difficult. How on earth could I manage to talk to Alice without being seen by the other members of her family?

As I halted on the slope, trying to work out what to do next, my problem was solved for me. A slim, dark figure came out of the back door of the farmhouse and began to climb the hill in my direction. It was Alice—but how had she known I was there? There were trees between the farmhouse and me, and the windows were facing in the wrong direction.

Still, she wasn't coming up the hill by chance. She walked straight up toward me and halted about five paces away.

"What do you want?" she asked. "You're stupid coming here. Lucky for you that those inside are asleep."

"I can't do what you asked," I said, holding out the basket toward her.

She folded her arms and frowned. "Why not?" she demanded. "You promised, didn't you?"

"You didn't tell me what would happen," I said. "She's eaten two cakes already and they're making her stronger. She's already bent the bars over the pit. One more cake and she'll be free and I think you know it. Wasn't that the idea all along?" I accused, starting to feel angry. "You tricked me, so the promise doesn't count anymore."

She took a step nearer, but now her own anger had been replaced by something else. Suddenly she looked scared.

"It wasn't my idea. They made me do it," she said, gesturing down toward the farmhouse. "If you don't do as you promised, it'll go hard with both of us. Go on, give her the third cake. What harm can it do? Mother Malkin's paid the price. It's time to let her go. Go on, give her the cake and she'll be gone tonight and never trouble you again."

"I think Mr. Gregory must've had a very good reason for putting her in that pit," I said slowly. "I'm just his new apprentice, so how can I know what's best? When he gets back I'm going to tell him everything that's happened."

Alice gave a little smile—the sort of smile someone gives when they know something that you don't. "He ain't coming back," she said. "Lizzie thought of it all. Got good friends near Pendle, Lizzie has. Do anything for her, they would. They tricked Old Gregory. When he's on the road he'll get what's coming to him. By now he's probably already dead and six feet under. You just wait and see if I'm right. Soon you won't be safe even up there in his house. One night they'll come for you. Unless, of course, you help now. In that case, they might just leave you alone."

As soon as she'd said that, I turned my back and climbed the hill, leaving her standing there. I think she called out to me several times, but I wasn't listening. What she'd said about the Spook was spinning around inside my head.

It was only later that I realized I was still carrying the basket, so I threw it and the last of the cakes into a river; then, back at the Spook's cottage, it didn't take me very long to work out what had happened and decide what to do next.

The whole thing had been planned from the start. They'd lured the Spook away, knowing that, as a new apprentice, I'd still be wet behind the ears and easy to trick.

I didn't believe that the Spook would be so easy to kill or he wouldn't have survived for so many years, but I couldn't rely on him arriving back in time to help me. Somehow I had to stop Mother Malkin from getting out of the pit.

I needed help badly and I thought of going down to the village, but I knew there was a more special kind of help near at hand. So I went into the kitchen and sat at the table.

At any moment I expected to have my ears boxed, so I talked quickly. I explained everything that had happened, leaving nothing out. Then I said that it was my fault and could I please be given some help.

I don't know what I expected. I didn't feel foolish talking to the empty air because I was so upset and frightened, but as the silence lengthened, I gradually realized that I'd been wasting my time. Why should the boggart help me? For all I knew it was a prisoner, bound to the house and garden by the Spook. It might just be a slave, desperate to be free; it might even be happy because I was in trouble.

Just when I was about to give up and leave the kitchen, I remembered something my dad often said before we went off to the local market: "Everyone has his price. It's just a case of making an offer that pleases him but doesn't hurt you too much."

So I made the boggart an offer.

"If you help me now, I won't forget it," I said. "When I become the next Spook, I'll give you every Sunday off. On that day I'll make my own meals so that you can have a rest and please yourself what you do."

Suddenly I felt something brush against my legs under the table. There was a noise, too, a faint purring, and a big ginger cat strolled into view and moved slowly toward the door.

It must have been under the table all the time—that's what common sense told me. I knew different, though, so I followed the cat out into the hallway and then up the stairs, where it halted outside the locked door of the library. Then it rubbed its back against it, the way cats do against table legs. The door slowly swung open to reveal more books than anyone could ever have read in one lifetime, arranged neatly on rows of parallel racks of shelves. I stepped inside, wondering where to begin. And when I turned around again, the big ginger cat had vanished.

Each book had its title neatly displayed on the cover. A lot were written in Latin and quite a few in Greek. There was no dust or cobwebs. The library was just as clean and well cared for as the kitchen.

I walked along the first row until something caught my eye. Near the window there were three very long shelves full of leather-bound notebooks, just like the one the Spook had given me, but the top shelf had larger books with dates on the covers. Each one seemed to record a period of five years, so I picked up the one at the end of the shelf and opened it carefully.

I recognized the Spook's handwriting. Flicking through the pages, I realized that it was a sort of diary. It recorded each job he'd done, the time taken in traveling and the amount he'd been paid. Most importantly, it explained just how each boggart, ghost, and witch had been dealt with.

I put the book back on the shelf and glanced along the other spines. The diaries extended almost up to the present day but went back hundreds of years. Either the Spook was a lot older than he looked or the earlier books had been written by other spooks who'd lived ages ago. I suddenly wondered whether, even if Alice was right and the Spook didn't come back, there was a possibility that I might be able to learn all I needed to know just by studying those diaries. Better still, somewhere in those thousands upon thousands of pages there might be information that would help me now.

How could I find it? Well, it might take time, but the witch had been in the pit for almost thirteen years. There had to be an account of how the Spook had put her there.

Then, suddenly, on a lower shelf, I saw something even better.

There were even bigger books, each dedicated to a particular topic. One was labeled *Dragons and Wormes*. As they were displayed in alphabetical order, it didn't take me long to find just what I was looking for.

Witches.

I opened it with trembling hands to find it was divided into four predictable sections. . . .

The Malevolent, The Benign, The Falsely Accused, and The Unaware.

I quickly turned to the first section. Everything was in the Spook's neat handwriting and, once again, carefully organized into alphabetical order. Within seconds I found a page titled "Mother Malkin."

It was worse than I'd expected. Mother Malkin was just about as evil as you could imagine. She'd lived in lots of places, and in each area she'd stayed, something terrible had happened, the worst thing of all occurring on a moss to the west of the County.

She'd lived on a farm there, offering a place to stay to young women who were expecting babies but had no husbands to support them. That was where she'd gotten the title "Mother." This had gone on for years, but some of the young women had never been seen again.

She'd had a son of her own living with her there, a young man of incredible strength called Tusk. He had big teeth and frightened people so much that nobody ever went near the place. But at last the locals had roused themselves, and Mother Malkin had been forced to flee to Pendle. After she'd gone, they'd found the first of the graves. There was a whole field of bones and rotting flesh, mainly the remains of the children she'd murdered to supply her need for blood. Some of the bodies were those of women; in each case the body had been crushed, the ribs broken or cracked.

The lads in the village had talked about a thing with too many teeth to fit in its mouth. Could that be Tusk, Mother Malkin's son? A son who'd probably killed those women by crushing the life out of them?

That set my hands trembling so much that I could hardly hold the book steady enough to read it. It seemed that some witches used bone magic. They were necromancers who got their power by summoning the dead. But Mother Malkin was even worse. Mother Malkin used blood magic. She got her power by using human blood and was particularly fond of the blood of children.

I thought of the black, sticky cakes and shuddered. A child had gone missing from the Long Ridge. A child too young to walk. Had it been snatched by Bony Lizzie? Had its blood been used to make those cakes? And what about the second child, the one the villagers were searching for? What if Bony Lizzie had snatched that one, too, ready for when Mother Malkin escaped from her pit so that she could use its blood to work her magic? The child might be in Lizzie's house now!

I forced myself to go on reading.

Thirteen years ago, early in the winter, Mother Malkin had come to live in Chipenden, bringing her granddaughter, Bony Lizzie, with her. When the Spook had come back from his winter house in Anglezarke, he'd wasted no time in dealing with her. After driving off Bony Lizzie, he'd bound Mother Malkin with a silver chain and carried her back to the pit in his garden.

The Spook seemed to be arguing with himself in the account. He clearly didn't like burying her alive but explained why it had to be done. He believed that it was too dangerous to kill her: once slain, she had the power to return and would be even stronger and more dangerous than before.

The point was, could she still escape? One cake and she'd been able to bend the bars. Although she wouldn't get the third, two might just be enough. At midnight she might still climb out of the pit. What could I do?

If you could bind a witch with a silver chain, then it might have been worth trying to fasten one across the top of the bent bars to stop her from climbing out of her pit. The trouble was, the Spook's silver chain was in his bag, which always traveled with him.

I saw something else as I left that library. It was beside

the door, so I hadn't noticed it as I came in. It was a long list of names on yellow paper, exactly thirty and all written in the Spook's own handwriting. My own name, Thomas J. Ward, was at the very bottom, and directly above it was the name William Bradley, which had been crossed out with a horizontal line; next to it were the letters *RIP*.

I felt cold all over then, because I knew that they meant Rest in Peace and that Billy Bradley had died. More than two thirds of the names on the paper had been crossed off; of those, nine besides Billy were dead.

I supposed that a lot were crossed out simply because they'd failed to make the grade as apprentices, perhaps not even making it to the end of the first month. Those who had died were more worrying. I wondered what had happened to Billy Bradley, and I remembered what Alice had said: *"You don't want to end up like Old Gregory's last apprentice."*

How did Alice know what had happened to Billy? It was probably just that everybody in the locality knew about it, while I was an outsider. Or had her family had something to do with it? I hoped not, but it gave me something else to worry about.

Wasting no more time, I went down to the village. The butcher seemed to have some contact with the Spook. How else had he gotten the sack to put the meat into? So I decided to tell him about my suspicions and try to persuade him to search Lizzie's house for the missing child.

It was late in the afternoon when I arrived at his shop, and it was closed. I knocked on the doors of five cottages before anyone came to answer. They confirmed what I already suspected: The butcher had gone off with the other men to search the fells. They wouldn't be back until noon the following day. It seemed that after searching the local fells, they were going to cross the valley to the village at the foot of the Long Ridge, where the first child had gone missing. There they'd carry out a wider search and stay overnight.

I had to face it. I was on my own.

Soon, both sad and afraid, I was climbing the lane back toward the Spook's house. I knew that if Mother Malkin got out of her grave, then the child would be dead before morning.

I knew also that I was the only one who might even try to do something about it.

CHAPTER IX
ON THE RIVERBANK

BACK at the cottage, I went to the room where the Spook kept his walking clothes. I chose one of his old cloaks. It was too big, of course, and the hem came down almost to my ankles, while the hood kept falling down over my eyes. Still, it would keep out the worst of the cold. I

· 173 ·

borrowed one of his staffs, too, the one most useful to me as a walking stick: It was shorter than the others and slightly thicker at one end.

When I finally left the cottage, it was close to midnight. The sky was bright and there was a full moon just rising above the trees, but I could smell rain and the wind was freshening from the west.

I walked out into the garden and headed directly for Mother Malkin's pit. I was afraid, but someone had to do it, and who else was there but me? It was all my fault anyway. If only I'd told the Spook about meeting Alice and what she'd told the lads about Lizzie being back! He could have sorted it all out then. He wouldn't have been lured away to Pendle.

The more I thought about it, the worse it got. The child on the Long Ridge might not have died. I felt guilty, so guilty, and I couldn't stand the thought that another child might die and that would be my fault, too.

I passed the second grave, where the dead witch was buried head down, and moved very slowly forward on my tiptoes until I reached the pit.

A shaft of moonlight fell through the trees to light it up, so there was no doubt about what had happened.

I was too late.

The bars had been bent even farther apart, almost into the shape of a circle. Even the butcher could have eased his massive shoulders through that gap.

I peered down into the blackness of the pit but couldn't see anything. I suppose I had a forlorn hope that she might have exhausted herself bending the bars and was now too tired to climb out.

Fat chance. At that moment a cloud drifted across the moon, making things a lot darker, but I could see the bent ferns. I could see the direction she'd taken. There was enough light to follow her trail.

So I followed her into the gloom. I wasn't moving too quickly, and I was being very, very cautious. What if she was hiding and waiting for me just ahead? I also knew that she probably hadn't gotten very far. For one thing, it wasn't more than five minutes or so after midnight. Whatever was in the cakes she'd eaten, I knew that dark magic would have played some part in getting her strength back. It was a magic that was supposed to be more powerful during the hours of darkness—particularly at midnight. She'd only eaten two cakes, not three, so that was in my favor, but I thought of the terrible strength needed to bend those bars.

Once out of the trees, I found it easy to follow her trail through the grass. She was heading downhill, but in a direction that would take her away from Bony Lizzie's cottage. That puzzled me at first, until I remembered the river in the gully below. A malevolent witch couldn't cross running water—the Spook had taught me that—so she would have to move along its banks until it curved back upon itself, leaving her way clear.

Once in sight of the river, I paused on the hillside and searched the land below. The moon came out from behind the cloud, but at first, even with its help, I couldn't see anything much down by the river because there were trees on both banks, casting dark shadows.

And then suddenly I noticed something very strange.

There was a silver trail on the near bank. It was only visible where the moon touched it, but it looked just like the glistening trail made by a snail. A few seconds later I saw a dark, shadowy thing, all hunched up, shuffling along very close to the riverbank.

I started off down the hill as quickly as I could. My intention was to cut her off before she reached the bend in the river and was able to head directly for Bony Lizzie's place. I managed that and stood there, the river on my right, facing downstream. But next came the difficult part. Now I had to face the witch.

I was trembling and shaking and so out of breath that you'd have thought I'd spent an hour or so running up and down the fells. It was a mixture of fear and nerves, and my knees felt as if they were going to give way any minute. It was only by leaning heavily on the Spook's staff that I was able to stay on my feet at all.

As rivers went, it wasn't that wide, but it was deep, swollen by the spring rains to a level where it had almost burst its banks. The water was moving fast, too, rushing away from me into the darkness beneath the trees where the witch was. I looked very carefully, but it still took me quite a few moments to find her.

Mother Malkin was moving in my direction. She was a shadow darker than the tree shadows, a sort of blackness that you could fall into, a darkness that would swallow you up forever. I heard her then, even above the noise made by the fast-flowing river. It wasn't just the sound of her bare feet, which were making a sort of slithery noise as they moved toward me through the long grass at the stream's edge. No—there were other sounds that she was making with her mouth and perhaps her nose. The same sort of noises she'd made when I'd fed her the cake. There were snortings and snufflings that once again brought into my mind the memory of our hairy pigs feeding from the swill bucket. Then a different sound, a sucking noise.

When she moved out from under the trees into the open, the moonlight fell on her and I saw her properly for the first time. Her head was bowed low, her face hidden by a tangled mass of white-and-gray hair, so it seemed that she was looking at her feet, which were just visible under the dark gown that came down to her ankles. She wore a black cloak, too, and either it was too long for her or the years she had spent in the damp earth had made her shrink. It hung down to the ground behind her, and it was this, dragging over the grass, that seemed to be making the silver trail.

Her gown was stained and torn, which wasn't really surprising, but some were fresh stains—dark, wet patches. Something was dripping onto the grass at her side, and the drips were coming from what she gripped tightly in her left hand.

It was a rat. She was eating a rat. Eating it raw.

She didn't seem to have noticed me yet. She was very close now, and if nothing happened, she'd bump right into me. I coughed suddenly. It wasn't to warn her. It was a nervous cough, and I hadn't meant it to happen.

She looked up at me then, lifting into the moonlight a face that was something out of a nightmare, a face that didn't belong to a living person. Oh, but she was alive all right. You could tell that by the noises she was making eating that rat.

But there was something else about her that terrified me so much that I almost fainted away on the spot. It was her eyes. They were like two hot coals burning inside their sockets, two red points of fire.

And then she spoke to me, her voice something between a whisper and a croak. It sounded like dry, dead leaves rustling together in a late autumn wind.

"It's a boy," she said. "I like boys. Come here, boy."

I didn't move, of course. I just stood there, rooted to the spot. I felt dizzy and light-headed.

She was still moving toward me and her eyes seemed to be growing larger. Not only her eyes; her whole body seemed to be swelling up. She was expanding into a vast cloud of darkness that within moments would darken my own eyes forever.

Without thinking, I lifted the Spook's staff. My hands and arms did it, not me.

"What's that, boy, a wand?" she croaked. Then she

chuckled to herself and dropped the dead rat, lifting both her arms toward me.

It was me she wanted. She wanted my blood. In absolute terror, my body began to sway from side to side. I was like a sapling agitated by the first stirrings of a wind, the first storm wind of a dark winter that would never end.

I could have died then, on the bank of that river. There was nobody to help, and I felt powerless to help myself.

But suddenly it happened. . . .

The Spook's staff wasn't a wand, but there's more than one kind of magic. My arms conjured up something special, moving faster than I could even think.

They lifted the staff and swung it hard, catching the witch a terrible blow on the side of the head.

She gave a sort of grunt and fell sideways into the river. There was a big splash, and she went right under but came up very close to the bank, about five or six paces downstream. At first I thought that that was the end of her, but to my horror, her left arm came out of the water and grabbed a tussock of grass. Then the other arm reached for the bank, and she started to drag herself out of the water.

I knew I had to do something before it was too late. So, using all my willpower, I forced myself to take a step toward her as she heaved more of her body up onto the bank.

When I got close enough, I did something that I can still remember vividly. I still have nightmares about it. But what choice did I have? It was her or me. Only one of us was going to survive.

I jabbed the witch with the end of the staff. I jabbed her hard, and I kept on jabbing her until she finally lost her grip on the bank and was swept away into the darkness.

But it still wasn't over. What if she managed to get out of the water farther downstream? She could still go to Bony Lizzie's house. I had to make sure that didn't happen. I knew it was the wrong thing to kill her and that one day she'd probably come back stronger than ever, but I didn't have a silver chain, so I couldn't bind her. It was now that mattered, not the future. No matter how hard it was, I knew I had to follow the river into the trees.

Very slowly I began to walk along the riverbank, pausing every five or six steps to listen. All I could hear was the wind sighing faintly through the branches above. It was very dark, with only the occasional thin shaft of moonlight managing to penetrate the leaf canopy, each like a long silver spear embedded in the ground.

The third time I paused, it happened. There was no warning. I didn't hear a thing. I simply felt it. A hand slithered up onto my boot, and before I could move away, it gripped my left ankle hard.

I felt the strength in that grip. It was as if my ankle were being crushed. When I looked down, all I could see was a pair of red eyes glaring up at me out of the darkness. Terrified, I jabbed down blindly toward the unseen hand that was clutching my ankle.

I was too late. My ankle was jerked violently and I fell to the ground, the impact driving all the breath from my body. What was worse, the staff went flying from my hand, leaving me defenseless.

I lay there for a moment or two, trying to catch my

breath, until I felt myself being dragged toward the river-bank. When I heard the splashing, I knew what was happening. Mother Malkin was using me to drag herself out of the river. The witch's legs were thrashing about in the water, and I knew that one of two things would happen: either she'd manage to get out, or I'd end up in the river with her.

Desperate to escape, I rolled over to my left, twisting my ankle away. She held on, so I rolled again and came to a halt with my face pressed against the damp earth. Then I saw the staff, its thicker end lying in a shaft of moonlight. It was out of reach, about three or four paces away.

I rolled toward it. Rolled again and again, digging my fingers into the soft earth, twisting my body like a corkscrew. Mother Malkin had a tight grip on my ankle, but that was all she had. The lower half of her body was still in the water, so despite her great strength, she couldn't stop me from rolling over and twisting her through the water after me.

At last I reached the staff and thrust it hard at the

witch. But her own hand moved into the moonlight and gripped the other end.

I thought it was over then. I thought that was the end of me, but to my surprise Mother Malkin suddenly screamed very loudly. Her whole body became rigid, and her eyes rolled up in her head. Then she gave a long, deep sigh and became very still.

We both lay there on the riverbank for what seemed a long time. Only my chest was rising and falling as I gulped in air; Mother Malkin wasn't moving at all. When, finally, she did, it wasn't to take a breath. Very slowly, one hand let go of my ankle and the other released the staff and she slid down the bank into the river, entering the water with hardly a splash. I didn't know what had happened, but she was dead—I was sure of it.

I watched her body being carried away from the bank by the current and swirled right into the middle of the river. Still lit by the moon, her head went under. She was gone. Dead and gone.

CHAPTER X
POOR BILLY

I WAS so weak afterward that I fell
to my knees, and within moments I
was sick—sicker than I'd ever been
before. I kept heaving and heaving
even when there was nothing but bile
coming out of my mouth, heaving until
my insides felt torn and twisted.

At last it ended and
I managed to

stand. Even then, it was a long time before my breathing slowed down and my body stopped trembling. I just wanted to go back to the Spook's house. I'd done enough for one night, surely?

But I couldn't—the child was in Lizzie's house. That was what my instincts told me. The child was the prisoner of a witch who was capable of murder. So I had no choice. There was nobody else but me, and if I didn't help, then who would? I had to set off for Bony Lizzie's house.

There was a storm surging in from the west, a dark jagged line of cloud that was eating into the stars. Very soon now it would begin to rain, but as I started down the hill toward the house, the moon was still out—a full moon, bigger than I ever remembered it.

It was casting my shadow before me as I went. I watched it grow, and the nearer I got to the house, the bigger it seemed to get. I had my hood up and I was carrying the Spook's staff in my left hand, so that the shadow didn't seem to belong to me anymore. It moved on ahead of me until it fell upon Bony Lizzie's house.

I glanced backward then, half expecting to see the Spook standing behind me. He wasn't there. It was just a trick of the light. So I went on until I'd passed through the open gate into the yard.

I paused before the front door to think. What if I was too late and the child was already dead? Or what if its disappearance was nothing to do with Lizzie and I was just putting myself in danger for nothing? My mind carried on thinking, but, just as it had on the riverbank, my body knew what to do. Before I could stop it, my left hand rapped the staff hard against the wood three times.

For a few moments there was silence, followed by the sound of footsteps and a sudden crack of light under the door.

As the door slowly swung open, I took a step backward. To my relief it was Alice. She was holding a lantern level with her head so that one half of her face was lit while the other was in darkness.

"What do you want?" she asked, her voice filled with anger.

"You know what I want," I replied. "I've come for the child. For the child that you've stolen."

"Don't be a fool," she said. "Go away before it's too late. They've gone off to meet Mother Malkin. They could be back any minute."

Suddenly a child began to cry, a thin wail coming from somewhere inside the house. So I pushed past Alice and went inside.

There was just a single candle flickering in the narrow passageway, but the rooms themselves were in darkness. The candle was unusual. I'd never seen one made of black wax before, but I snatched it up anyway and let my ears guide me to the right room.

I eased open the door. The room was empty of furniture, and the child was lying on the floor on a heap of straw and rags.

"What's your name?" I asked, trying my best to smile. I leaned my staff against the wall and moved closer.

The child stopped crying and tottered to its feet, its eyes very wide. "Don't worry. There's no need to be scared," I said, trying to put as much reassurance into my voice as possible. "I'm going to take you home to your mam."

I put the candle on the floor and picked up the child. It smelled as bad as the rest of the room, and it was cold and wet. I cradled it with my right arm and wrapped my cloak about it as best I could.

Suddenly the child spoke. "I'm Tommy," it said. "I'm Tommy."

"Well, Tommy," I said, "we've got the same name. My name's Tommy, too. You're safe now. You're going home."

With those words, I picked up my staff and went into the passageway and out through the front door. Alice was standing in the yard near the gate. The lantern had gone out, but the moon was still shining, and as I walked nearer, it threw my shadow onto the side of the barn, a giant shadow ten times bigger than I was.

I tried to pass her, but she stepped directly into my path so that I was forced to halt.

"Don't meddle!" she warned, her voice almost a snarl, her teeth gleaming white and sharp in the moonlight. "Ain't none of your business, this."

I was in no mood to waste time arguing with her, and when I moved directly toward her, Alice didn't try to stop me. She stepped back out of my way and called out after me, "You're a fool. Give it back before it's too late. They'll come after you. You'll never get away."

I didn't bother to answer. I never even looked back. I went through the gate and began to climb away from the house.

It started to rain then, hard and heavy, straight into my face. It was the kind of rain that my dad used to call wet rain. All rain is wet, of course, but some kinds do seem to make a better and a faster job of soaking you than others. This was as wet as it got, and I headed back toward the Spook's house as fast as I could.

I wasn't sure if I'd be safe even there. What if the Spook really was dead? Would the boggart still guard his house and garden?

Soon I had more immediate things to worry about. I began to sense that I was being followed. The first time I felt it, I came to a halt and listened, but there was nothing but the howling of the wind and the rain lashing into the trees and drumming onto the earth. I couldn't see much either, because it was very dark now.

So I carried on, taking even bigger strides, just hoping that I was still heading in the right direction. Once I came up against a thick, high hawthorn hedge and had to make a long detour to find a gate, all the time feeling that the danger behind was getting closer. It was just after I'd come through a small wood that I knew for certain that there was someone there. Climbing a hill, I paused for breath close to its summit. The rain had eased for a moment and I looked back down into the darkness, toward the trees. I heard the crack and snap of twigs. Someone was moving very fast through the wood in my direction, not caring where he put his feet.

At the crest of the hill I looked back once more. The first flash of lightning lit up the sky and the ground below, and I saw two figures come out of the trees and begin to climb the slope. One of them was female, the other shaped like a man, big and burly.

When the thunder crashed again, Tommy began to cry. "Don't like thunder!" he wailed. "Don't like thunder!"

"Storms can't hurt you, Tommy," I told him, knowing it wasn't true. They scared me as well. One of my uncles had been struck by lightning when he'd been out trying to get some cattle in. He'd died later. It wasn't safe being out in the open in weather like this. But although lightning terrified me, it did have its uses. It was showing me the way, each vivid flash lighting up my route back to the Spook's house.

Soon the breath was sobbing in my throat, too, a mixture of fear and exhaustion, as I forced myself to go faster and faster, just hoping that we'd be safe as soon as we entered the Spook's garden. Nobody was allowed on the Spook's property unless invited — I kept telling myself that over and over again, because it was our only chance. If we could just get there first, the boggart would protect us.

I was in sight of the trees, the bench beneath them, the garden waiting beyond, when I slipped on the wet grass. The fall wasn't hard, but Tommy began to cry even louder. When I'd managed to pick him up, I heard someone running behind me, feet thumping the earth.

I glanced back, struggling for breath. It was a mistake. My pursuer was about five or six paces ahead of Lizzie and catching me fast. Lightning flashed again, and I saw the lower half of his face. It looked as if he had horns growing out of each side of his mouth, and as he ran he moved his head from side to side. I remembered what I'd read in the Spook's library about the dead women who'd been found with their ribs crushed. If Tusk caught me, he'd do the same to me.

For a moment I was rooted to the spot, but he started to make a bellowing sound, just like a bull, and that started me moving again. I was almost running now. I would have sprinted if I could, but I was carrying Tommy and I was too weary, my legs heavy and sluggish, the breath rasping in my throat. At any moment I expected to be grabbed from behind, but I passed the bench where the Spook often gave me lessons and then, at last, I was beneath the first trees of the garden.

But was I safe? If I wasn't, it was all over for both of us, because there was no way I could outrun Tusk to the house. I stopped running, and all I could manage was a few steps before I came to a complete halt, trying to regain my breath.

It was at that moment that something brushed past my legs. I looked down, but it was too dark to see anything. First I felt the pressure, then I heard something purr, a deep throbbing sound that made the ground beneath my feet vibrate. I sensed it move on beyond me, toward the edge of the trees, positioning itself between us and those who'd been following. I couldn't hear any running now, but I heard something else.

Imagine the angry howl of a tomcat multiplied a hundred times. It was a mixture between a throbbing growl and a scream, filling the air with its warning challenge, a sound that could have been heard for miles. It was the most terrifying and threatening sound I'd ever heard, and I knew then why the villagers never came anywhere near the Spook's house. That cry was filled with death.

Cross this line, it said, *and I'll rip out your heart. Cross this line, and I'll gnaw your bones to pulp and gore. Cross this line, and you'll wish you'd never been born.*

So for now we were safe. By now Bony Lizzie and Tusk would be running back down the hill. Nobody would be foolish enough to tangle with the Spook's boggart. No wonder they'd needed me to feed Mother Malkin the blood cakes.

There was hot soup and a blazing fire waiting for us in the kitchen. I wrapped little Tommy in a warm blanket and fed him some soup. Later I brought down a couple of pillows and made up a bed for him close to the fire. He slept like a log while I listened to the wind howling outside and the rain pattering against the windows.

It was a long night, but I was warm and comfortable and I felt at peace in the Spook's house, which was one of the safest places in the whole wide world. I knew now that nothing unwelcome could even enter the garden, never mind cross the threshold. It was safer than a castle with high battlements and a wide moat. I began to think of the boggart as my friend, and a very powerful friend at that.

Just before noon I carried Tommy down to the village. The men were already back from the Long Ridge, and when I went to the butcher's house, the instant he saw the child, his weary frown turned into a broad smile. I briefly explained what had happened, only going into as much detail as was necessary.

Once I'd finished, he frowned again. "They need sorting out once and for all," he said.

I didn't stay long. After Tommy had been given to his mother and she'd thanked me for the fifteenth time, it became obvious what was going to happen. By then, about thirty or so of the village men had gathered. Some of them were carrying clubs and stout sticks and they were muttering angrily about stoning and burning.

I knew that something had to be done, but I didn't

want to be a part of it. Despite all that had happened, I couldn't stand the thought of Alice being hurt, so I went for a walk on the fells for an hour or so to clear my head before walking slowly back toward the Spook's house. I'd decided to sit on the bench for a while and enjoy the afternoon sun, but someone was there already.

It was the Spook. He was safe after all! Until that moment I'd avoided thinking about what I was going to do next. I mean, how long would I have stayed in his house before deciding that he wasn't going to come back? Now it was all sorted out because there he was, staring across the trees to where a plume of brown smoke was rising. They were burning Bony Lizzie's house.

When I got close to the bench, I noticed a big, purple bruise over his left eye. He saw me glance at it and gave me a tired smile.

"We make a lot of enemies in this job," he said, "and sometimes you need eyes in the back of your head. Still, things didn't work out too badly because now we've one less enemy to worry about near Pendle.

"Take a pew," he said, patting the bench at his side. "What have you been up to? Tell me what's been happening here. Start at the beginning and finish at the end, leaving nothing out."

So I did. I told him everything. When I'd finished he stood up and looked down at me, his green eyes staring into mine very hard.

"I wish I'd known Lizzie was back. When I put Mother Malkin into the pit, Lizzie left in a bit of a hurry and I didn't think she'd ever have the nerve to show her face again. You should have told me about meeting the girl. It would have saved everybody a lot of trouble."

I looked down, unable to meet his eyes.

"What was the worst thing that happened?" he asked.

The memory came back, sharp and clear, of the old witch grabbing my boot and trying to drag herself out of the water. I remembered her scream as she gripped the end of the Spook's staff.

When I told him about it, he sighed long and deep.

"Are you sure she was dead?" he asked.

I shrugged. "She wasn't breathing. Then her body was carried to the middle of the river and swept away."

"Well, it was a bad business, all right," he said, "and the memory of it will stay with you for the rest of your life, but you'll just have to live with it. You were lucky in taking the smallest of my staffs with you. That's what saved you in the end. It's made of rowan, the most effective wood of all when dealing with witches. It wouldn't usually have bothered a witch that old and that strong, but she was in running water. So you were lucky, but you did all right for a new apprentice. You showed courage, real courage, and you saved a child's life. But you made two more serious mistakes."

I bowed my head. I thought I'd probably made more than two, but I wasn't going to argue.

"Your most serious mistake was in killing that witch," the Spook said. "She should have been brought back here. Mother Malkin is so strong that she could even break free of her bones. It's very rare, but it can happen. Her spirit could be born into this world again, complete with all her memories. Then she'd come looking for you, lad, and she'd want revenge."

"That would take years though, wouldn't it?" I asked. "A newborn baby can't do much. She'd have to grow up first."

"That's the worst part of it," the Spook said. "It could happen sooner than you think. Her spirit could seize someone else's body and use it as her own. It's called possession, and it's a bad business for everybody concerned. After that, you'll never know when, and from which direction, the danger will come.

"She might possess the body of a young woman, a lass with a dazzling smile, who'll win your heart before she takes your life. Or she might use her beauty to bend some strong man to her will, a knight or a judge, who'll have you thrown into a dungeon where you'll be at her mercy. Then again, time will be on her side. She might attack when I'm not here to help—maybe years from now when you're long past your prime, when your eyesight's failing and your joints are starting to creak.

"But there's another type of possession—one that's more likely in this case. Much more likely. You see, lad, there's a problem with keeping a live witch in a pit like that. Especially one so powerful, who's spent her long life practicing blood magic. She'll have been eating worms and other slithery things, with the wet constantly soaking into her flesh. So in the same way that a tree can slowly be petrified and turned into rock, her body will have been slowly starting to change. Gripping the rowan staff would have stopped her heart, pushing her over the barrier into death, and being washed away by the river might have speeded up the process.

"In this case, she'll still be bound to her bones, like most other malevolent witches, but because of her great strength, she'll be able to move her dead body. You see, lad, she'll be what we call wick. It's an old County word that you're no doubt familiar with. Just as a head of hair can be wick with lice, her dead body is now wick with her wicked spirit. It'll be heaving like a bowl of maggots and she'll crawl, slither, or drag herself toward her chosen victim. And instead of being hard, like a petrified tree, her dead body will be soft and pliable, able to squeeze into the tiniest space. Able to ooze up someone's nose or into his ear and possess his body.

"There are only two ways to make sure that a witch as powerful as Mother Malkin can't come back. The first is to burn her. But nobody should have to suffer pain like that. The other way is too horrible even to think about. It's a method few have heard about because it was practiced long ago, in a land far away over the sea. According to their ancient books, if you eat the heart of a witch, she can never return. And you have to eat it raw.

"If we practice either method, we're no better than the witch we kill," said the Spook. "Both are barbaric. The only alternative left is the pit. That's cruel as well, but we do it to protect the innocents, those who'd be her future victims. Well, lad, one way or the other, now she's free. There's trouble ahead for sure, but there's little we can do about it now. We'll just have to be on our guard."

"I'll be all right," I said. "I'll manage somehow."

"Well, you'd better start by learning how to manage a boggart," the Spook said, shaking his head sadly.

"That was your other big mistake. A whole Sunday off every week? That's far too generous! Anyway, what should we do about that?" he asked, gesturing toward a thin plume of smoke that was still just visible to the southeast.

I shrugged. "I suppose it'll be all over by now," I said. "There were a lot of angry villagers, and they were talking about stoning."

"All over with? Don't you believe it, lad. A witch like Lizzie has a sense of smell better than any hunting dog. She can sniff out things before they happen and would've been gone long before anyone got near. No, she'll have fled back to Pendle, where most of the brood live. We should follow now, but I've been on the road for days, and I'm too weary and sore and need to gather my strength. But we can't leave Lizzie free for too long, or she'll start to work her mischief again. I'll have to go after her before the end of the week, and you'll be coming with me. It won't be easy, but you might as well get used to the idea. But first things first, so follow me. . . ."

As I followed, I noticed that he had a slight limp and was walking more slowly than usual. So whatever had happened on Pendle, it hadn't been without cost to himself. He led me into the house, up the stairs, and into the library, halting beside the farthest shelves, the ones near the window.

"I like to keep my books in my library," he said, "and I like my library to get bigger rather than smaller. But because of what's happened, I'm going to make an exception."

He reached up and took a book from the very top shelf and handed it to me. "You need this more than I do," he said. "A lot more."

As books went, it wasn't very big. It was even smaller than my notebook. Like most of the Spook's books, it was bound in leather and had its title printed both on the front cover and on the spine. It said *Possession: The Damned, the Dizzy, and the Desperate.*

"What does the title mean?" I asked.

"What it says, lad. Exactly what it says. Read the book and you'll find out."

When I opened the book, I was disappointed. Inside, every word on every page was printed in Latin, a language I couldn't read.

"Study it well and carry it with you at all times," said the Spook. "It's the definitive work."

He must have seen me frowning, because he smiled and jabbed at the book with his finger. "Definitive means that so far it's the best book that's ever been written about possession, but it's a very difficult subject and it was written by a young man who still had a lot to learn. So it's not the last word on the subject, and there's more to discover. Turn to the back of the book."

I did as he told me and found that the last ten or so pages were blank.

"If you find out anything new, then just write it down there. Every little bit helps. And don't worry about the fact that it's in Latin. I'll be starting your lessons as soon as we've eaten."

We went for our afternoon meal, which was cooked almost to perfection. As I swallowed down my last mouthful, something moved under the table and began to rub itself against my legs. Suddenly the sound of purring could be heard. It gradually got louder and louder until all the plates and dishes on the sideboard began to rattle.

"No wonder it's happy," said the Spook, shaking his head. "One day off a year would have been nearer the mark! Still, not to worry, it's business as usual and life goes on. Bring your notebook with you, lad, we've a lot to get through today."

So I followed the Spook down the path to the bench, uncorked the bottle of ink, dipped in my pen, and prepared to take notes.

"Once they've passed the test in Horshaw," said the Spook, starting to limp up and down in front of the bench, "I usually try to ease my apprentices into the job as gently as possible. But now that you've been face-to-face with a witch, you know how difficult and dangerous the job can be, and I think you're ready to find out what happened to my last apprentice. It's linked to boggarts, the topic we've been studying, so you might as well learn from it. Find a clean page and write down this for a heading . . ."

I did as I was told. I wrote down *How to Bind a Boggart*. Then, as the Spook told the tale, I took notes, struggling to keep up as usual.

As I already knew, binding a boggart involved a lot of hard work which the Spook called "laying." First a pit had to be dug as close as possible to the roots of a large, mature tree. After all the digging the Spook had made me do, I was surprised to learn that a spook rarely dug the pit himself. That was something only done in an absolute emergency. A rigger and his helper usually attended to it.

Next you had to employ a mason to cut a thick slab of stone to fit over the pit like a gravestone. It was very important that the stone be cut to size accurately so as to make a good seal. After you'd coated the lower edge of the stone and the inside of the pit with the mixture of iron, salt, and strong glue, it was time to get the boggart safely inside.

That wasn't too difficult. Blood, milk, or a combination of the two worked every time. The really difficult bit was dropping the stone into position as it fed. Success depended on the quality of the help you hired.

It was best to have a mason standing by and a couple of riggers using chains controlled from a wooden gantry placed above the pit, so as to lower the stone down quickly and safely.

That was the mistake that Billy Bradley made. It was late winter and the weather was foul and Billy was in a rush to get back to his warm bed. So he cut corners.

He used local laborers, who hadn't done that type of work before. The mason had gone off for his supper, promising to return within the hour, but Billy was impatient and couldn't wait. He got the boggart into the pit without too much trouble, but he ran into difficulties with the slab of stone. It was a wet night, and it slipped, trapping his left hand under its edge.

The chain jammed so they couldn't lift the stone, and while the laborers struggled with it and one of them ran back to get the mason, the boggart, in a fury at being trapped under the stone, began to attack Billy's fingers. You see, it was one of the most dangerous boggarts of all: cattle rippers that had got the taste for human blood.

By the time the stone was lifted, almost half an hour had passed, and by then it was too late. The boggart had bitten off Billy's fingers as far down as the second knuckle and had been busily sucking the blood from his body. Billy's screams of pain had faded away to a whimper, and when they got his hand free, only his thumb was left. Soon afterward he died of shock and loss of blood.

"It was a sad business," said the Spook, "and now he's buried under the hedge, just outside the churchyard at Layton—those who follow our trade don't get to rest their bones in hallowed ground. It happened just over a year ago, and if Billy had lived, I wouldn't be talking to you now, because he'd still be my apprentice. Poor Billy, he was a good lad and he didn't deserve that, but it's a dangerous job and if it's not done right . . ."

The Spook looked at me sadly, then shrugged. "Learn

from it, lad. We need courage and patience, but above all, we never rush. We use our brains, we think carefully, then we do what has to be done. In the normal course of events I never send an apprentice out on his own until his first year of training is over. Unless, of course," he added with a faint smile, "he takes matters into his own hands. Then again, I've got to feel sure he's ready for it. Anyway, now it's time for your first Latin lesson. . . ."

CHAPTER XI
THE PIT

IT happened just three days later.

The Spook had sent me down into the village to collect the week's groceries. It was very late in the afternoon, and as I left his house carrying the empty sack, the shadows were already beginning to lengthen.

As I approached the stile, I saw someone standing right on the edge of

· 215 ·

the trees near the top of the narrow lane. When I realized that it was Alice, my heart lurched into a more rapid beat. What was she doing here? Why hadn't she gone off to Pendle? And if she was still here, what about Lizzie?

I slowed down, but I had to pass her to get to the village. I could've gone back and taken a longer route, but I didn't want to give her the satisfaction of thinking I was scared of her. Even so, once I'd climbed over the stile, I stayed on the left-hand side of the lane, keeping close to the high hawthorn hedge, right on the edge of the deep ditch that ran along its length.

Alice was standing in the gloom, with just the toes of her pointy shoes poking out into the sunlight. She beckoned me closer, but I kept my distance, staying a good three paces away. After all that had happened, I didn't trust her one little bit, but I was still glad that she hadn't been burned or stoned.

"I've come to say good-bye," Alice said, "and warn you never to go walking near Pendle. That's where we're going. Lizzie has family living there."

"I'm glad you escaped," I said, coming to a halt and turning to face directly toward her. "I watched the smoke when they burned your house down."

"Lizzie knew they were coming," Alice said, "so we got away with plenty of time to spare. Didn't sniff you out, though, did she? Knows what you did to Mother Malkin, but only found out after it happened. Didn't sniff you out at all, and that worries her. And she said your shadow had a funny smell."

I laughed out loud at that. I mean, it was crazy. How could a shadow have a smell?

"Ain't funny," Alice accused. "Ain't nothing to laugh at. She only smelled your shadow where it had fallen on the barn. I actually saw it, and it was all wrong. The moon showed the truth of you."

Suddenly she took two steps nearer, into the sunlight, then leaned forward a little and sniffed at me. "You do smell funny," she said, wrinkling up her nose. She stepped backward quickly and suddenly looked afraid.

I smiled and put on my friendly voice. "Look," I said,

REVENGE *Of* THE WITCH

"don't go to Pendle. You're better off without them. They're just bad company."

"Bad company don't matter to me. Won't change me, will it? I'm bad already. Bad inside. You wouldn't believe the things I've been and done. I'm sorry," she said. "I've been bad again. I'm just not strong enough to say no—"

Suddenly, too late, I understood the real reason for the fear on Alice's face. It wasn't me she was scared of. It was what was standing right behind me.

I'd seen nothing and heard nothing. When I did, it was already too late. Without warning, the empty sack was snatched out of my hand and dropped over my head and shoulders, and everything went dark. Strong hands gripped me, pinning my arms to my sides. I struggled for a few moments, but it was useless: I was lifted and carried as easily as a farmhand carries a sack of potatoes. While I was being carried, I heard voices—Alice's voice and then the voice of a woman; I supposed it was Bony Lizzie. The person carrying me just grunted, so it had to be Tusk.

Alice had lured me into a trap. It had all been carefully

planned. They must have been hiding in the ditch as I came down the hill from the house.

I was scared, more scared than I'd ever been in my life before. I mean, I'd killed Mother Malkin, and she'd been Lizzie's grandmother. So what were they going to do to me now?

After an hour or so I was dropped onto the ground so hard that all the air was driven from my lungs.

As soon as I could breathe again, I struggled to get free of the sack, but somebody thumped me twice in the back—thumped me so hard that I kept very still. I'd have done anything to avoid being hit like that again, so I lay there, hardly daring to breathe while the pain slowly faded to a dull ache.

They used rope to tie me then, binding it over the sack, around my arms and head and knotting it tightly. Then Lizzie said something that chilled me to the bone.

"There, we've got him safe enough. You can start digging now."

Her face came very close to mine, so that I could smell her foul breath through the sacking. It was like the breath of a dog or a cat. "Well, boy," she said. "How does it feel to know that you'll never see the light of day again?"

When I heard the sound of distant digging, I began to shiver with fright. I remembered the Spook's tale of the miner's wife, especially the worst bit of all when she'd laid there paralyzed, unable to cry out while her husband dug her grave. Now it was going to happen to me. I was going to be buried alive, and I'd have done anything just to see daylight again, even for a moment.

At first, when they cut my ropes and pulled the sack from me, I was relieved. By then the sun had gone down, but I looked up and could see the stars, with the waning moon low over the trees. I felt the wind on my face, and it had never felt so good. My feeling of relief didn't last more than a few moments, though, because I started to wonder exactly what they had in mind for me. I couldn't think of anything worse than being buried alive, but Bony Lizzie probably could.

To be honest, when I saw Tusk close up for the first time, he wasn't quite as bad as I expected. In a way he'd looked worse the night he was chasing me. He wasn't as old as the Spook, but his face was lined and weather-beaten, and a mass of greasy gray hair covered his head. His teeth were too big to fit into his mouth, which meant that he could never close it properly, and two of them curved upward like yellow tusks on either side of his nose. He was big, too, and very hairy, with powerful, muscular arms. I'd felt that grip and had thought it bad enough, but I knew that he had the power in those shoulders to squeeze me so tightly that all the air would be forced from my body and my ribs would shatter.

Tusk had a big curved knife at his belt, with a blade that looked very sharp. But the worst thing about him was his eyes. They were completely dull. It was as if there was nothing alive inside his head; he was just something that obeyed Bony Lizzie without even a thought. I knew that he'd do anything she told him without question, no matter how terrible it was.

As for Bony Lizzie, she wasn't skinny at all, and I knew, from my reading in the Spook's library, that she was probably called that because she used bone magic. I'd already smelled her breath, but at a glance you'd never have taken her for a witch. She wasn't like Mother Malkin, all shriveled with age, looking like something that was already dead. No, Bony Lizzie was just an older version of Alice. Probably no older than thirty-five, she had pretty brown eyes and hair as black as her niece's. She wore a green shawl and a black dress fastened neatly at her slim waist with a narrow leather belt. There was certainly a family resemblance—except for her mouth. It wasn't the shape of it, it was the way she moved it; the way it twisted and sneered when she talked. One other thing I noticed was that she never looked me in the eye.

Alice wasn't like that. She had a nice mouth, still shaped for smiling, but I realized then that she would eventually become just like Bony Lizzie.

Alice had tricked me. She was the reason I was here

rather than safe and sound back in the Spook's house, eating my supper.

At a nod from Bony Lizzie, Tusk grabbed me and tied my hands behind my back. Then he seized me by the arm and dragged me through the trees. First of all I saw the mound of dark soil, then the deep pit beside it, and I smelled the wet, loamy stink of freshly turned earth. It smelled sort of dead and alive at the same time, with things brought to the surface that really belonged deep underground.

The pit was probably more than seven feet deep, but unlike the one the Spook had kept Mother Malkin in, it was irregular in shape, just a great big hole with steep sides. I remember thinking that with all the practice I'd had, I could have dug one far better.

At that moment the moon showed me something else—something I'd have preferred not to see. About three paces away, to the left of the pit, there was an oblong of freshly turned soil. It looked just like a new grave.

Without time even to begin worrying about that, I was dragged right to the edge of the pit, and Tusk forced my head back. I had a glimpse of Bony Lizzie's face close to mine, something hard was jammed into my mouth, and a cold, bitter-tasting liquid was poured down my throat. It tasted vile and filled my throat and mouth to the brim, spilling over and even erupting out of my nose so that I began to choke, gasping and struggling for breath. I tried to spit it out, but Bony Lizzie pinched my nostrils hard with her finger and thumb, so that in order to breathe I first had to swallow.

That done, Tusk let go of my head and transferred his grip back to my left arm. I saw then what had been forced into my mouth — Bony Lizzie held it up for me to see. It was a small bottle made out of dark glass. A bottle with a long, narrow neck. She turned it so that its neck was pointing to the ground and a few drops fell to the earth. The rest was already in my stomach.

What had I drunk? Had she poisoned me?

"That'll keep your eyes wide open, boy," she said with

a sneer. "Wouldn't want you dozing off, would we? Wouldn't want you to miss anything."

Without warning, Tusk swung me around violently toward the pit, and my stomach lurched as I fell into space. I landed heavily, but the earth at the bottom was soft and although the fall winded me, I was unhurt. So I turned to look up at the stars, thinking that maybe I was going to be buried alive after all. But instead of a shovelful of dirt falling toward me, I saw the outline of Bony Lizzie's head and shoulders peering down, a silhouette against the stars. She started to chant in a strange sort of throaty whisper, though I couldn't catch the actual words.

Next she stretched her arms out above the pit, and I could see that she was holding something in each hand. Giving a strange cry, she opened her hands and two white things dropped toward me, landing in the mud close to my knees.

By the moonlight I saw clearly what they were. They almost seemed to be glowing. She'd dropped two bones into the pit. They were thumb bones—I could see the knuckles.

"Enjoy your last night on this earth, boy," she called down to me. "But don't worry, you won't be lonely because I'll leave you in good company. Dead Billy will be coming to claim his bones. Just next door, he is, so he's not got too far to go. He'll be with you soon, and you two have a lot in common. He was Old Gregory's last apprentice, and he won't take kindly to you having taken his place. Then, just before dawn, we'll be paying you one last visit. We'll be coming to collect your bones. They're special, your bones are, even better than Billy's, and taken fresh they'll be the most useful I've had for a long time."

Her face drew back, and I heard footsteps walking away.

So that was what was going to happen to me. If Lizzie wanted my bones, it meant that she was going to kill me. I remembered the big curved blade that Tusk wore at his belt, and I began to tremble.

Before that I had Dead Billy to face. When she'd said, "just next door," she must have meant the new grave next to the pit. But the Spook had said that Billy Bradley was buried just outside the churchyard at Layton. Lizzie must have dug up his body, cut off his thumbs, and buried the rest of him here among the trees. Now he'd be coming to get his thumbs back.

Would Billy Bradley want to hurt me? I'd never done him any harm, but he'd probably enjoyed being the Spook's apprentice. Maybe he'd looked forward to finishing his time and becoming a spook himself. Now I'd taken what he once had. Not only that—what about Bony Lizzie's spell? He might think I was the one who'd cut off his thumbs and thrown them into the pit. . . .

I managed to kneel up and spent the next few minutes desperately trying to untie my hands. It was hopeless. My struggles seemed to be making the rope even tighter.

I felt strange, too: light-headed and dry mouthed. When I looked up at the stars, they seemed to be very bright and each star had a twin. If I concentrated hard, I could make the double stars become single again, but as soon as I relaxed, they drifted apart. My throat was burning and my heart pounding three or four times faster than its normal pace.

I kept thinking about what Bony Lizzie had said. Dead Billy would be coming to find his bones. Bones that were lying in the mud less than two paces from where I was kneeling. If my hands had been free, I'd have hurled those bones from the pit.

Suddenly I saw a slight movement to my left. Had I been standing, it would've been just about level with my head. I looked up and watched as a long, plump, white, maggoty head emerged from the side of the pit. It was far, far bigger than any worm I'd ever seen before. Its blind, bloated head moved in a slow circle as it wriggled out the rest of its body. What could this be? Was it poisonous? Could it bite?

And then it came to me. It was a coffin worm! It must be something that had been living in Billy Bradley's coffin, growing fat and sleek. Something white that had never seen the light of day!

I shuddered as the coffin worm wriggled out of the

dark earth and plopped into the mud at my feet. I lost sight of it then as it quickly burrowed beneath the surface.

Being so big, the white worm had dislodged quite a bit of soil from the side of the pit, leaving behind a hole like a narrow tunnel. I watched it, horrified but fascinated, because there was something else moving inside it. Something disturbing the earth, which was cascading from the hole to form a growing mound of soil.

Not knowing what it was made it worse. I had to see what was inside, so I struggled to get to my feet. I staggered, feeling light-headed again, the stars starting to spin. I almost fell, but I managed to take a step, lurching forward so that I was close to the narrow tunnel, now just about level with my head.

When I looked inside, I wished I hadn't.

I saw bones. Human bones. Bones that were joined together. Bones that were moving. Two hands without thumbs. One of them without fingers. Bones squelching in the mud, dragging themselves toward me through the soft earth. A grinning skull with gaping teeth.

It was Dead Billy, but instead of eyes, his black sockets stared back at me, cavernous and empty. When a white, fleshless hand emerged into the moonlight and jerked at my face, I stepped away, nearly falling, sobbing with fear.

At that moment, just when I thought I might go out of my mind with terror, the air suddenly became much colder and I sensed something to my right. Someone else had joined me in the pit. Someone who was standing where it was impossible to stand. Half his body was on view; the rest was embedded in the wall of earth.

It was a boy not much older than me. I could only see his left-hand side because the rest of him was somewhere behind, still in the soil. Just as easily as stepping through a door, he swung his right shoulder toward me and the rest of him entered the pit. He smiled at me. A warm, friendly smile.

"The difference between waking and dreaming," he said. "That's one of the hardest lessons to learn. Learn it now, Tom. Learn it now before it's too late. . . ."

For the first time I noticed his boots. They looked very

expensive and had been crafted from best-quality leather. They were just like the Spook's.

He lifted his hands up then, so that they were at each side of his head, palms facing outward. The thumbs were missing from each hand. His left hand was also without fingers.

It was the ghost of Billy Bradley.

He crossed his hands over his chest and smiled once more. As Billy faded away, he seemed happy and at peace.

I understood exactly what he'd told me. No, I wasn't asleep, but in a way I'd been dreaming. I'd been dreaming the dark dreams that had come out of the bottle that Lizzie had forced into my mouth.

When I turned back to look at the hole, it was gone. There never had been a skeleton crawling toward me. Neither had there been a coffin worm.

The potion must have been some kind of poison: something that made it difficult to tell the difference between waking and dreaming. That was what Lizzie had given me. It had made my heart beat faster and made it impossible for me to sleep. It had kept my eyes wide open, but it had also made them see things that weren't really there.

Soon afterward the stars disappeared and it began to rain heavily. It was a long, uncomfortable, cold night and I kept thinking about what would happen to me before dawn. The nearer it got, the worse I felt.

About an hour before sunrise, the rain eased to a light drizzle before fading away altogether. Once more I could see the stars, and by now they no longer seemed double. I was soaked and cold, but my throat had stopped burning.

When a face appeared overhead looking down into the pit, my heart began to race because I thought it was Lizzie come to collect my bones. But, to my relief, it was Alice.

"Lizzie's sent me to see how you're getting on," she called down softly. "Has Billy been yet?"

"He's been and gone," I told her angrily.

"I never meant for this to happen, Tom. If only you hadn't meddled, it would have been all right."

"Been all right?" I said. "By now another child would be dead and the Spook, too, if you'd had your way. And those cakes had the blood of a baby inside. Do you call that being all right? You come from a family of murderers and you're a murderer yourself!"

"Ain't true. It ain't true, that!" Alice protested. "There was no baby. All I did was give you the cakes."

"Even if that were so," I insisted, "you knew what they were going to do afterward. And you would've let it happen."

"I ain't that strong, Tom. How could I stop it? How could I stop Lizzie?"

"I've chosen what I want to do," I told her. "But what will you choose, Alice? Bone magic or blood magic? Which one? Which one will it be?"

"Ain't going to do either. I don't want to be like them. I'll run away. As soon as I get the chance, I'll be off."

"If you mean that, then help me now. Help me get out

of the pit. We could run away together."

"It's too dangerous now," Alice said. "I'll run away later. Maybe weeks from now when they ain't expecting it."

"You mean after I'm dead. When you've got more blood on your hands . . ."

Alice didn't reply. I heard her begin to cry softly, but just when I thought she was on the verge of changing her mind and helping me, she walked away.

I sat there in the pit, dreading what was going to happen to me, remembering the hanging men and now knowing exactly how they must have felt before they died. I knew that I'd never go home. Never see my family again. I'd just about given up all hope when footsteps approached the pit. I came to my feet, terrified, but it was Alice again.

"Oh, Tom, I'm sorry," she said. "They're sharpening their knives. . . ."

The worst moment of all was approaching, and I knew that I only had one chance. The only hope I had was Alice.

"If you're really sorry, then you'll help me," I said softly.

"Ain't nothing I can do," she cried. "Lizzie could turn on me. She don't trust me. Thinks I'm soft."

"Go and fetch Mr. Gregory," I said. "Bring him here."

"Too late for that, ain't it?" Alice sobbed, shaking her head. "Bones taken in daylight are no use to Lizzie. No use at all. The best time to take bones is just before the sun comes up. So they'll be coming for you in a few minutes. That's all the time you've got."

"Then get me a knife," I said.

"No use, that," she said. "Too strong, they are. Can't fight 'em, can you?"

"No," I said. "I want it to cut the rope. I'm going to run for it."

Suddenly Alice was gone. Had she gone to fetch a knife, or would she be too scared of Lizzie? I waited a few moments, but when she didn't come back I became desperate. I struggled, trying to pull my wrists apart, trying to snap the rope, but it was no use.

When a face peered down at me, my heart jumped

with fear, but it was Alice holding something out over the pit. She dropped it, and as it fell, metal gleamed in the moonlight.

Alice hadn't let me down. It was a knife. If I could just cut the rope, I'd be free. . . .

At first, even with my hands tied behind my back, I never had any doubt in my mind that I could do it. The only danger was that I might cut myself a bit, but what did that matter compared to what they'd do to me before the sun came up? It didn't take me long to get a grip on the knife. Positioning it against the rope was more difficult, and it was very hard to move it. When I dropped it for the second time, I began to panic. There couldn't be more than a minute or so before they came for me.

"You'll have to do it for me," I called up to Alice. "Come on, jump down into the pit."

I didn't think she'd really do it, but to my surprise she did. She didn't jump but lowered herself down feet first, facing the side of the pit and hanging on to the edge with her arms. When her body was fully extended, she dropped the final two feet or so.

It didn't take her long to cut the rope. My hands were free, and all we had to do was get out of the pit.

"Let me stand on your shoulders," I said. "Then I'll pull you up."

Alice didn't argue, and at the second attempt I managed to balance on her shoulders and drag myself up onto the wet grass. Then came the really hard part — pulling Alice out of the pit.

I reached down with my left hand. She gripped it hard with her own and placed her right hand on my wrist for extra support. Then I tried to pull her up.

My first problem was the wet, slippery grass, and I found it hard to keep myself from being dragged over the edge. Then I realized that I didn't have the strength to do it. I'd made a big mistake. Just because she was a girl, that didn't necessarily make her weaker than me. Too late I remembered the way she'd pulled the rope to make the Spook's bell dance. She'd done it almost effortlessly. I should have let her stand on my shoulders. I should have let her get out of the pit first. Alice would have pulled me up without any trouble.

It was then that I heard the sound of voices. Bony Lizzie and Tusk were coming through the trees toward us.

Below me I saw Alice's feet scrabbling against the side of the pit, trying to get a hold. Desperation gave me extra strength. I gave a sudden heave, and she came up over the edge and collapsed beside me.

We got away just in time, running hard with the sound of other feet running behind us. They were quite a long way back at first, but very gradually they began to get closer and closer.

I don't know how long we ran. It felt like a lifetime. I ran until my legs felt like lead and the breath was burning in my throat. We were heading back toward Chipenden — I could tell that from the occasional glimpses I got of the fells through the trees. We were running toward the dawn. The sky was graying now and growing lighter by the minute. Then, just as I felt I couldn't take another step, the tips of the fells were glowing a pale orange. It was sunlight, and I remember thinking that even if we were caught now, at least it was daylight and so my bones would be of no use to Lizzie.

As we came out of the trees onto a grassy slope and began to run up it, my legs finally began to fail. They were turning to jelly, and Alice was starting to pull away from me. She glanced back at me, her face terrified. I could still hear them crashing through the trees behind us.

Then I came to a complete and sudden halt. I stopped because I wanted to stop. I stopped because there was no need to run any farther.

There, standing at the summit of the slope ahead, was a tall figure dressed in black, carrying a long staff. It was the Spook, all right, but somehow he looked different. His hood was thrown back and his hair, lit by the rays of the rising sun, seemed to be streaming back from his head like orange tongues of flame.

Tusk gave a sort of roar and ran up the slope toward

him, brandishing his blade, with Bony Lizzie close at his heels. They weren't bothered about us for the moment. They knew who their main enemy was. They could deal with us later.

By now Alice had come to a halt, too, so I took a couple of shaky steps to bring myself level with her. We both watched as Tusk made his final charge, lifting his curved blade and bellowing angrily as he ran.

The Spook had been standing as still as a statue, but then in response he took two big strides down the slope toward him and lifted his staff high. Aiming it like a spear, he drove it hard at Tusk's head. Just before it made contact with his forehead, there was a sort of click and a red flame appeared at the very tip. There was a heavy thud as it struck home. The curved knife went up in the air, and Tusk's body fell like a sack of potatoes. I knew he was dead even before he hit the ground.

Next the Spook cast his staff to one side and reached inside his cloak. When his left hand appeared again, it was clutching something that he cracked high in the air like a whip. It caught the sun, and I knew it was a silver chain.

Bony Lizzie turned and tried to run, but it was too late: The second time he cracked the chain, it was followed almost immediately by a thin, high, metallic sound. The chain began to fall, shaping itself into a spiral of fire to bind itself tightly around Bony Lizzie. She gave one great shriek of anguish, then fell to the ground.

I walked with Alice to the summit of the slope. There we saw that the silver chain was wrapped tightly about the witch from head to toe. It was even tight across her open mouth, hard against her teeth. Her eyes were rolling in her head and her whole body was twitching with effort, but she couldn't cry out.

I glanced across at Tusk. He was lying on his back with his eyes wide open. He was dead, all right, and there was a red wound in the middle of his forehead. I looked at the staff then, wondering about the flame I'd seen at its tip.

My master looked gaunt, tired, and suddenly very

old. He kept shaking his head as if he were weary of life itself. In the shadow of the slope, his hair was back to its usual gray color, and I realized why it had seemed to stream back from his head: It was saturated with sweat and he'd slicked it back with his hand so that it stuck up and out behind his ears. He did it again as I watched. Beads of sweat were dripping from his brow, and he was breathing very rapidly. I realized he'd been running.

"How did you find us?" I asked.

It was a while before he answered, but at last his breathing began to slow and he was able to speak. "There are signs, lad. Trails that can be followed, if you know how. That's something else you'll have to learn."

He turned and looked at Alice. "That's two of them dealt with, but what are we going to do about you?" he asked, staring at her hard.

"She helped me escape," I said.

"Is that so?" asked the Spook. "But what else did she do?"

He looked hard at me then, and I tried to hold his gaze. When I looked down at my boots, he made a clicking noise with his tongue. I couldn't lie to him, and I knew that he'd guessed that she'd played some part in what had happened to me.

He looked at Alice again. "Open your mouth, girl," he said harshly, his voice full of anger. "I want to see your teeth."

Alice obeyed, and the Spook suddenly reached forward, seizing her by the jaw. He brought his face close to her open mouth and sniffed very loudly.

When he turned back to me, his mood seemed to have softened, and he gave a deep sigh. "Her breath is sweet enough," he said. "You've smelled the breath of the other?" he asked, releasing Alice's jaw and pointing down at Bony Lizzie.

I nodded.

"It's caused by her diet," he said. "And it tells you right away what she's been up to. Those who practice bone or blood magic get a taste for blood and raw meat. But the girl seems all right."

Then he moved his face close to Alice's again. "Look

into my eyes, girl," he told her. "Hold my gaze as long as you can."

Alice did as he told her, but she couldn't look at him for long, even though her mouth was twitching with the effort. She dropped her eyes and began to cry softly.

The Spook looked down at her pointy shoes and shook his head sadly. "I don't know," he said, turning at me again. "I just don't know what to do for the best. It's not just her. We've others to think about. Innocents who might suffer in the future. She's seen too much and she knows too much for her own good. It could go either way with her, and I don't know if it's safe to let her go. If she goes east to join the brood at Pendle, then she'll be lost forever and she'll just add to the dark."

"Haven't you anywhere else you could go?" I asked Alice gently. "No other relations?"

"There's a village near the coast. It's called Staumin. I've another aunt lives there. Perhaps she'd take me in . . ."

"Is she like the others?" the Spook asked, staring at Alice again.

"Not so you'd notice," she replied. "Still, it's a long way and I ain't ever been there before. Could take three days or more to get there."

"I could send the lad with you," said the Spook, his voice suddenly a lot kinder. "He's had a good look at my maps, so I reckon he should be able to find the way. When he gets back, he'll be learning how to fold them up properly. Anyway, it's decided. I'm going to give you a chance, girl. It's up to you whether you take it. If you don't, then one day we'll meet again, and the next time you won't be so lucky."

Then the Spook pulled the usual cloth from his pocket. Inside it was a hunk of cheese for the journey. "Just so you don't go hungry," he said, "but don't eat it all at once."

I hoped we might find something better to eat on the way, but I still mumbled my thanks.

"Don't go straight to Staumin," said the Spook, staring at me hard without blinking. "I want you to go home again first. Take this girl with you, and let your mother talk to her. I've a feeling she might just be able to help. I'll expect you back within two weeks."

That brought a smile to my face. After all that had happened, a chance to go home for a while was a dream come true. But one thing did puzzle me, because I remembered the letter my mam had sent the Spook. He hadn't seemed that happy with some of the things she'd said. So why should he think my mam would be able to help Alice? I didn't say anything, because I didn't want to risk making the Spook have second thoughts. I was just glad to be away.

Before we left, I told him about Billy. He nodded sadly but said not to worry because he'd do what was necessary.

As we set off, I glanced back and saw the Spook carrying Bony Lizzie over his left shoulder and striding away toward Chipenden. From behind you'd have taken him for a man thirty years younger.

CHAPTER XII
THE DESPERATE AND THE DIZZY

As we came down the hill toward the farm, warm drizzle was drifting into our faces. Somewhere far off a dog barked twice, but below us everything was quiet and still.

It was late afternoon, and I knew that my dad and Jack would be out in the fields, which would give me a chance to talk to Mam alone. It was easy for the Spook to tell me to take Alice home with me, but the journey had given me time to think, and I didn't know how Mam would take it. I didn't feel she'd be happy having someone like Alice in the house, especially when I told her what she'd been up to. And as for Jack, I'd a pretty good idea what his reaction would be. From what Ellie had told me last time about his attitude to my new job, having the niece of a witch in the house was the last thing he'd want.

As we crossed the yard I pointed to the barn. "Better shelter under there," I said. "I'll go in and explain."

No sooner had I spoken than the loud cry of a hungry baby came from the direction of the farmhouse. Alice's eyes met mine briefly, then she looked down, and I remembered the last time we'd been together when a child had cried.

Without a word, Alice turned and walked into the barn, her silence no more than I expected. You'd think that after all that had happened, there'd have been a lot to talk about on the journey, but we'd hardly spoken. I think she'd been upset by the way the Spook had held her by the jaw and smelled her breath. Maybe it had made her think about all the things she'd been up to in the past. Whatever it was, she'd seemed deep in thought and very sad for most of the time.

I suppose I could have tried harder, but I was too tired and weary, so we'd walked in silence until it had grown into a habit. It was a mistake: I should have made the effort to get to know Alice better then—it might have saved me a lot of trouble later.

As I jerked open the back door, the crying stopped and I heard another sound, the comforting click of Mam's rocking chair.

The chair was by the window, but the curtains weren't fully drawn, and I could see by her face that she'd been peering through the narrow gap between them. She'd watched us enter the yard, and as I came into the room, she began to rock the chair faster and harder, staring at me all the while without blinking, one half of her face in darkness, the other lit by the large candle that was flickering in its big brass holder in the center of the table.

"When you bring a guest with you, it's good manners to invite her into the house," she said, her voice a mixture of annoyance and surprise. "I thought I'd taught you better than that."

"Mr. Gregory told me to bring her here," I said. "Her name's Alice, but she's been keeping bad company. He wants you to talk to her but I thought it was best to tell you what's happened first, just in case you didn't want to invite her in."

So I drew up a chair and told Mam exactly what had happened. When I'd finished she let out a long sigh, then a faint smile softened her face.

"You've done well, son," she told me. "You're young and new to the job, so your mistakes can be forgiven. Go and bring that poor girl in, then leave us alone to talk. You might want to go upstairs and say hello to your new niece. Ellie will certainly be glad to see you."

So I brought Alice in, left her with my mam, and went upstairs.

Ellie was in the biggest bedroom. It used to belong to my mam and dad, but they'd let her and Jack have it because there was room for another two beds and a cot, which would come in useful as their family grew.

I knocked lightly on the door, which was half open, but only looked into the room when Ellie called out for me to go in. She was sitting on the edge of the big double bed feeding the baby, its head half hidden by her pink shawl. As soon as she saw me, her mouth widened into a smile that made me feel welcome, but she looked tired and her hair lank and greasy. Although I glanced away quickly, Ellie was sharp and I knew she'd seen me staring and read the expression in my eyes, because she quickly smoothed the hair away from her brow.

"Oh, I'm sorry, Tom," she said. "I must look a mess—I've been up all night. I've just grabbed an hour's sleep. You've got to get it while you can with a very hungry baby like this. She cries a lot, especially at night."

"How old is she?" I asked.

"She'll be just six days old tonight. She was born not long after midnight last Saturday."

That was the night I'd killed Mother Malkin. For a moment the memory of it came rushing back and a shiver ran down my spine.

"Here, she's finished feeding now," Ellie said with a smile. "Would you like to hold her?"

That was the last thing I wanted to do. The baby was so small and delicate that I was scared of squeezing it too hard or dropping it, and I didn't like the way its head was so floppy. It was hard to say no, though, because Ellie would have been hurt. As it was, I didn't have to hold the baby for long, because the moment it was in my arms its little face went red and it began to cry.

"I don't think it likes me," I told Ellie.

"She's a *she*, not an *it*," Ellie scolded, making her face all stern and outraged. "Don't worry, it's not you, Tom," she said, her mouth softening into a smile. "I think she's still hungry, that's all."

The baby stopped crying the moment Ellie took her

back, and I didn't stay long after that. Then, on my way downstairs, I heard a sound from the kitchen I hadn't expected.

It was laughter, the loud, hearty laughter of two people getting on very well together. The moment I opened the door and walked in, Alice's face became very serious, but Mam carried on laughing aloud for a few moments, and even when she stopped, her face was still lit up with a wide smile. They'd been sharing a joke, a very funny joke, but I didn't like to ask what it was and they didn't tell me. The look in both their eyes made me feel that it was something private.

My dad once told me that women know things that men don't. That sometimes they have a certain look in their eyes, but when you see it, you should never ask them what they're thinking. If you do, they might tell you something you don't want to hear. Well, whatever they'd been laughing at had certainly brought them closer; from that moment on it seemed as if they'd known each other for years. The Spook had been right.

If anyone could sort Alice out, it had to be Mam.

I did notice one thing, though. Mam gave Alice the room opposite hers and Dad's. They were the two rooms at the top of the first flight of stairs. Mam had very sharp ears, and it meant that if Alice so much as turned over in her sleep, she would hear it.

So for all that laughter, Mam was still watching Alice.

When he came back from the fields, Jack gave me a really dark scowl and muttered to himself. He seemed angry at something. But Dad was pleased to see me, and to my surprise he shook hands with me. He always shook hands when greeting my other brothers who'd left home, but this was the first time for me. It made me feel sad and proud at the same time. He was treating me as if I were a man, making my own way in the world.

Jack hadn't been in the house five minutes when he came looking for me. "Outside," he said, keeping his voice low so that nobody else could hear. "I want to talk to you."

We walked out into the yard and he led the way around the side of the barn, close to the pigpens, where we couldn't be seen from the house.

"Who's the girl you've brought back with you?"

"Her name's Alice. It's just someone who needs help," I said. "The Spook told me to bring her home so that Mam could talk to her."

"What do you mean, she needs help?"

"She's been keeping bad company, that's all."

"What sort of bad company?"

I knew he wouldn't like it, but I had no choice. I had to tell him. Otherwise he'd only ask Mam.

"Her aunt's a witch, but don't worry—the Spook's sorted it all out and we'll only be staying for a few days."

Jack exploded. I'd never seen him so angry.

"Don't you have the sense you were born with?" he shouted. "Didn't you think? Didn't you think about the baby? There's an innocent child living in this house, and you bring home someone from a family like that! It's beyond belief!"

He raised his fist and I thought he was going to thump me. Instead, he smashed it sideways into the wall of the barn, the sudden thud sending the pigs into a frenzy.

"Mam thinks it's all right," I protested.

"Aye, Mam would," said Jack, his voice suddenly lower but still harsh with anger. "How could she refuse her favorite son anything? And she's just too good-hearted, as well you know. That's why you shouldn't take advantage. Look, it's me you'll answer to if anything happens. I don't like the look of that girl. She looks shifty. I'll be watching her carefully, and if she takes one step out of line, you'll both be on your way before you can blink. And you'll earn your keep while you're here. She can help around the house to make things easier for Mam, and you can pull your weight with the farmwork."

Jack turned and started to walk away, but he still had more to say. "Being so occupied with more important things," he added sarcastically, "you might not have noticed how tired Dad looks. He's finding the job harder and harder."

"Of course I'll help," I called after him, "and so will Alice."

⊙ ⊙ ⊙

At supper, apart from Mam, everyone was really quiet. I suppose it was having a stranger sitting at the table with us. Although Jack's manners wouldn't let him complain outright, he scowled at Alice almost as much as he did at me. So it was a good job Mam was cheerful and bright enough to light up the whole table.

Ellie had to leave her supper twice to attend to the baby, which kept crying fit to bring the roof down. The second time she fetched it downstairs.

"Never known a baby to cry so much," said Mam with a smile. "At least it's got strong, healthy lungs."

Its tiny face was all red and screwed up again. I would never have said it to Ellie, but it wasn't the best looking of babies. Its face reminded me of an angry little old woman. One moment it was crying fit to burst; then, very suddenly, it became still and quiet. Its eyes were wide open and it was staring toward the center of the table, where Alice was seated close to the big brass candlestick. At first I didn't think anything of it. I thought Ellie's baby was just fascinated by the candle flame. But later Alice helped Mam clear the table, and each time Alice passed by, the baby followed her with its blue eyes, and suddenly, although the kitchen was warm, I shivered.

Later I went up to my old bedroom, and when I sat down in the wicker chair by the window and gazed out, it was as if I'd never left home.

As I looked northward, toward Hangman's Hill, I thought about the way the baby had seemed so interested in Alice. When I remembered what Ellie had said earlier, I shivered again. Her baby had been born after midnight on the night of the full moon. It was too close to be just a coincidence. Mother Malkin would have been swept away by the river about the time that Ellie's baby had been born. The Spook had warned me that she'd come back. What if she'd come back even earlier than he'd predicted? He expected her to be wick. But what if he was wrong? What if she'd broken free of her bones and her spirit had possessed Ellie's baby at the very moment of its birth?

❍ ❍ ❍

I didn't sleep a wink that night. There was only one person I could talk to about my fears, and that was Mam. The difficulty was in getting her alone without drawing attention to the fact that I was doing it.

Mam cooked and did other chores that kept her busy most of the day, and usually it would have been no problem to talk to her in the kitchen because I was working close by. Jack had given me the job of repairing the front of the barn, and I must have hammered in hundreds of shiny new nails before sunset.

Alice was the difficulty, though: Mam kept her with her all day, really making the girl work hard. You could see the sweat on her brow and the frowns that kept furrowing her forehead, but despite that, Alice never complained even once.

It was only after supper, when they'd finished the clatter of washing and drying the dishes, that I finally got my chance. That morning Dad had gone off to the big spring market in Topley. He could conduct his business, and it gave him a rare chance to meet up with a few of his old friends, so he'd be away for two or three days. Jack was right. He did look tired, and it would give him a break from the farm.

Mam had sent Alice off to her room to get some rest, Jack had his feet up in the front room, and Ellie was upstairs trying to grab half an hour's sleep before the baby woke again for feeding. So, wasting no time at all, I started to tell Mam what was worrying me. She'd been rocking in her chair, but I'd hardly managed to blurt out my first sentence before the chair came to a halt. She listened carefully as I told her of my fears and reasons to suspect the baby. But her face remained so still and calm that I'd no idea what she was thinking. No sooner had I spat out my last word than she rose to her feet.

"Wait there," she said. "We need to sort this out once and for all."

She left the kitchen and went upstairs. When she came back she was carrying the baby, wrapped in Ellie's shawl. "Bring the candle," she said, moving toward the door.

We went out into the yard, Mam walking fast, as if she knew exactly where she was going and what she was going to do. We ended up at the other side of the cattle midden, standing in the mud on the edge of our pond, which was deep enough and large enough to provide water for our cows even through the driest summer months.

"Keep the candle high so we can see everything," Mam said. "I want there to be no doubt."

Then, to my horror, she stretched out her arms and held the baby over the dark, still water. "If she floats, the witch is inside her," Mam said. "If she sinks, she's innocent. Right, let's see —"

"No!" I shouted, my mouth opening all by itself and the words just tumbling out faster than I could think. "Don't do it, please. It's Ellie's baby."

For a moment I thought she was going to let the baby fall anyway, then she smiled and held it close again and kissed it on the forehead very gently. "Of course it's Ellie's baby, son. Can't you tell that just by looking at her? Anyway, swimming is a test carried out by fools and doesn't work anyway. Usually they tie the poor woman's hands to her feet and throw her into deep, still water. But whether she sinks or floats depends on luck and the kind of body she has. It's nothing to do with witchcraft."

"What about the way the baby kept staring at Alice?" I asked.

Mam smiled and shook her head. "A newborn baby's eyes aren't able to focus properly," she explained. "It was probably just the light of the candle that caught her attention. Remember — Alice was sitting close to it. Later, each time Alice passed by, the baby's eyes would just have been drawn by the change in the light. It's nothing. Nothing to worry about at all."

"But what if Ellie's baby is possessed anyway?" I asked. "What if there's something inside her that we can't see?"

"Look, son, I've delivered both good and evil into this world, and I know evil just by looking at it. This is a good child, and there's nothing inside her to worry about. Nothing at all."

"Isn't it strange, though, that Ellie's baby should be born about the same time that Mother Malkin died?"

"Not really," Mam answered. "It's the way of things. Sometimes, when something bad leaves the world, something good enters in its place. I've seen it happen before."

Of course, I realized then that Mam had never even considered dropping the baby and had just been trying to shock some sense into me, but as we walked back across the yard, my knees were still trembling with the thought of it. It was then, as we reached the kitchen door, that I remembered something.

"Mr. Gregory gave me a little book all about possession," I said. "He told me to read it carefully, but the trouble is, it's written in Latin and I've only had three lessons so far."

"It's not my favorite language," Mam said, pausing by the door. "I'll see what I can do, but it'll have to wait until I get back — I'm expecting to be called away tonight. In the meantime, why don't you ask Alice? She might be able to help."

○ ○ ○

Mam was right about being called away. A cart came for her just after midnight, the horses all in a sweat. It seemed that a farmer's wife was having a really bad time of it and had already been in labor for more than a day and a night. It was a long way as well, almost twenty miles to the south. That meant that Mam would be away for a couple of days or more.

I didn't really want to ask Alice to help with the Latin. You see, I knew the Spook would have disapproved. After all, it was a book from his library and he wouldn't have liked the idea of Alice even touching it. Still, what choice did I have? Since coming home, I'd been thinking about Mother Malkin more and more, and I just couldn't get her out of my mind. It was just an instinct, just a feeling, but I felt that she was somewhere out there in the dark and she was getting nearer with each night that passed.

So the following night, after Jack and Ellie had gone to bed, I tapped softly on Alice's bedroom door. It wasn't something I could ask her during the day because she was always busy, and if Ellie or Jack overheard, they wouldn't like it. Especially with Jack's dislike of spook's business.

I had to rap twice before Alice opened the door. I'd been worried that she might already be in bed asleep, but she still hadn't undressed and I couldn't stop my eyes from glancing down at her pointy shoes. On the dressing table there was a candle set close to the mirror. It had just been blown out—it was still smoking.

"Can I come in?" I asked, holding my own candle high so that it lit her face from above. "There's something I need to ask you."

Alice nodded me inside and closed the door.

"I've a book that I need to read, but it's written in Latin. Mam said you might be able to help."

"Where is it?" Alice asked.

"In my pocket. It's only a small book. For anyone who knows Latin, reading it shouldn't take that long."

Alice gave a deep, weary sigh. "I'm busy enough as it is," she complained. "What's it about?"

"Possession. Mr. Gregory thinks Mother Malkin could come back to get me and that she'll use possession."

"Let's see it then," she asked, holding out her hand. I placed my candle next to hers, then reached into my breeches and pulled out the small book. She skimmed through the pages without a word.

"Can you read it?" I asked.

"Don't see why not. Lizzie taught me, and she knows her Latin backward."

"So you'll help me?"

She didn't reply. Instead she brought the book very close to her face and sniffed it loudly. "You sure this is any good?" she asked. "Written by a priest, this is, and they don't usually know that much."

"Mr. Gregory called it the definitive work," I said, "which means it's the best book ever written on the subject."

She looked up from the book then, and to my surprise her eyes were filled with anger. "I know what definitive means," she said. "Think I'm stupid or something? Studied for years, I have, while you've only just started.

Lizzie had lots of books, but they're all burned now. All gone up in flames."

I muttered that I was sorry, and she gave me a smile.

"Trouble is," she said, her voice suddenly softening, "reading this'll take time, and I'm too tired to start now. Tomorrow your mam'll still be away, and I'll be as busy as ever. That sister-in-law of yours has promised to help, but she'll mostly be busy with the baby, and the cooking and cleaning will take me most of the day. But if you were to help . . ."

I didn't know what to say. I'd be helping Jack, so I wouldn't have much free time. The trouble was, men never did any cooking or cleaning, and it wasn't just that way on our farm. It was the same everywhere in the County. Men worked on the farm, outdoors in all weathers, and when they came in, the women had a hot meal waiting on the table. The only time we ever helped in the kitchen was on Christmas Day, when we did the washing up as a special treat for Mam.

It was as if Alice could read my mind, because her

smile grew wider. "Won't be too hard, will it?" she asked. "Women feed the chickens and help with the harvest, so why shouldn't men help in the kitchen? Just help me with the washing up, that's all. And some of the pans'll need scouring before I start cooking."

So I agreed to what she wanted. What choice did I have? I only hoped that Jack wouldn't catch me at it. He'd never understand.

I got up even earlier than usual and managed to scour the pans before Jack came down. Then I took my time over breakfast, eating very slowly, which was unlike me and enough to draw at least one suspicious glance from Jack. After he'd gone off into the fields, I washed the pots as quickly as I could and set to drying them. I might have guessed what would happen, because Jack never had much patience.

He came into the yard cursing and swearing and saw me through the window, his face all screwed up in disbelief. Then he spat into the yard and came around and pulled open the kitchen door with a jerk.

"When you're ready," he said sarcastically, "there's *men's* work to be done. And you can start by checking and repairing the pigpens. Snout's coming tomorrow. There are five to be slaughtered, and we don't want to spend all our time rounding up strays."

Snout was our nickname for the pig butcher, and Jack was right. Pigs sometimes panicked when Snout got to work, and if there was any weakness in the fence they'd find it for sure.

Jack turned to stamp away and then suddenly cursed loudly. I went to the door to see what was the matter. He'd accidentally stepped on a big fat toad, squashing it to a pulp. It was supposed to be bad luck to kill a frog or a toad, and Jack cursed again, frowning so much that his black bushy eyebrows met in the middle. He kicked the dead toad under the drain spout and went off, shaking his head. I couldn't think what had got into him. Jack never used to be so bad tempered.

I stayed behind and dried up every last pot—as he'd

caught me at it, I might as well finish the job. Besides, pigs stank and I wasn't much looking forward to the job that Jack had given me.

"Don't forget the book," I reminded Alice as I opened the door to leave, but she just gave me a strange smile.

I didn't get to speak to Alice alone again until late that night, after Jack and Ellie had gone off to bed. I thought I'd have to visit her room again, but instead she came down into the kitchen carrying the book and sat herself down in Mam's rocking chair, close to the embers of the fire.

"Made a good job of those pans, you did. Must be desperate to find out what's in here," Alice said, tapping the spine of the book.

"If she comes back, I want to be ready. I need to know what I can do. The Spook said she'll probably be wick. Do you know about that?"

Alice's eyes widened and she nodded.

"So I need to be ready. If there's anything in that book that can help, I need to know about it."

"This priest ain't like the others," Alice said, holding the book out toward me. "Mostly knows his stuff, he does. Lizzie would love this more than midnight cakes."

I pushed the book into my breeches pocket and drew up a stool on the other side of the hearth, facing what was left of the fire. Then I started to question Alice. At first it was really hard work. She didn't volunteer much, and what I did manage to drag out of her just made me feel a lot worse.

I began with the strange title of the book. *Possession. The Damned, the Dizzy, and the Desperate.* What did it mean? Why call the book that?

"First word is just priest talk," Alice said, turning down the corners of her mouth in disapproval. "They just use 'damned' for people who do things differently. For people like your mam, who don't go to church and say the right prayers. People who aren't like them. People who are left-handed," she said, giving me a knowing smile.

"Second word's more useful," Alice continued. "A

body that's newly possessed has poor balance. It keeps falling over. Takes time, you see, for the possessor that's moved in to fit itself comfortably into its new body. It's like trying to wear in a new pair of shoes. Makes it bad tempered, too. Someone calm and placid can strike out without warning. So that's another way you can tell.

"Then, as for the third word, that's easy. A witch who once had a healthy human body is desperate to get another one. Then, once she succeeds, she's desperate to hold on to it. Ain't going to give it up without a fight. She'll do anything. Anything at all. That's why the possessed are so dangerous."

"If she came here, who would it be?" I asked. "If she were wick, who would she try to possess? Would it be me? Would she try to hurt me that way?"

"Would if she could," Alice said. "Ain't easy though, what with you being what you are. Like to use me, too, but I won't give her the chance. No, she'll go for the weakest. The easiest."

"Ellie's baby?"

"No, that ain't no use to her. She'd have to wait till it's all grown up. Mother Malkin never had much patience, and being trapped in that pit at Old Gregory's would have made her worse. If it's you she's coming to hurt, first she'll get herself a strong, healthy body."

"Ellie then? She'll choose Ellie!"

"Don't you know anything?" Alice said, shaking her head in disbelief. "Ellie's strong. She'd be difficult. No, men are much easier. Especially a man whose heart always rules his head. Someone who can fly into a temper without even thinking."

"Jack?"

"It'll be Jack for sure. Think what it'd be like to have big strong Jack after you. But the book's right about one thing. A body that's newly possessed is easier to deal with. Desperate it is, but dizzy, too."

I got my notebook out and wrote down anything that seemed important. Alice didn't talk as fast as the Spook, but after a bit she got into her stride and it wasn't long before my wrist was aching. When it came to the really important business—how to deal with the possessed—there were lots of reminders that the original soul was still trapped inside the body. So if you hurt the body, you hurt that innocent soul as well. So just killing the body to get rid of the possessor was as bad as murder.

In fact that section of the book was disappointing: There didn't seem to be a lot you could do. Being a priest, the writer thought that an exorcism, using candles and holy water, was the best way to draw out the possessor and release the victim, but he admitted that not all priests could do it and that very few could do it really well. It seemed to me that some of the priests who could do it were probably seventh sons of seventh sons and that was what really mattered.

After all that, Alice said she felt tired and went up to bed. I was feeling sleepy, too. I'd forgotten how hard farmwork could be and I was aching from head to foot. Once up in my room, I sank gratefully onto my bed, anxious to sleep. But down in the yard the dogs had started to bark.

Thinking that something must have alarmed them, I

opened the window and looked out toward Hangman's Hill, taking a deep breath of night air to steady myself and clear my head. Gradually the dogs became quieter and eventually stopped barking altogether.

As I was about to close the window, the moon came out from behind a cloud. Moonlight can show the truth of things—Alice had told me that—just as that big shadow of mine had told Bony Lizzie that there was something different about me. This wasn't even a full moon, just a waning moon shrinking down to a crescent, but it showed me something new, something that couldn't be seen without it. By its light, I could see a faint silver trail winding down Hangman's Hill. It crept under the fence and across the north pasture, then crossed the eastern hay field until it vanished from sight somewhere behind the barn. I thought of Mother Malkin then. I'd seen the silver trail the night I'd knocked her into the river. Now here was another trail that looked just the same, and it had found me.

My heart thudding in my chest, I tiptoed downstairs

and slipped out through the back door, closing it carefully behind me. The moon had gone behind a cloud, so when I went around to the back of the barn, the silver trail had vanished, but there was still clear evidence that something had moved down the hill toward our farm buildings. The grass was flattened as if a giant snail had slithered across it.

I waited for the moon to reappear so that I could check the flagged area behind the barn. A few moments later the cloud blew away and I saw something that really scared me. The silver trail gleamed in the moonlight, and the direction it had taken was unmistakable. It avoided the pigpen and snaked around the other side of the barn in a wide arc to reach the far edge of the yard. Then it moved toward the house, ending directly under Alice's window, where the old wooden hatch covered the steps that led down to the cellar.

A few generations back, the farmer who'd lived here used to brew ale, which he'd supplied to the local farms and even a couple of inns. Because of that, the locals called our farm Brewer's Farm, although we just called it home. The steps were there so that barrels could be taken in and out without having to go through the house.

The hatch was still in place covering the steps, a big rusty padlock holding its two halves in position, but there was a narrow gap between them, where the two edges of the wood didn't quite meet. It was a gap no wider than my thumb, but the silver trail ended exactly there, and I knew that whatever had slithered toward this point had somehow slipped through that tiny gap. Mother Malkin was back and she was wick, her body soft and pliable enough to slip through the narrowest of gaps.

She was already in the cellar.

We never used the cellar now, but I remembered it well enough. It had a dirt floor, and it was mostly full of old barrels. The walls of the house were thick and hollow, which meant that soon she could be anywhere inside the walls, anywhere in the house.

I glanced up and saw the flicker of a candle flame in the window of Alice's room. She was still up. I went inside, and moments later I was standing outside her bedroom door. The trick was to tap just loud enough to let Alice know I was there without waking anybody else. But as I held my knuckles close to the door, ready to knock, I heard a sound from inside the room.

I could hear Alice's voice. She seemed to be talking to someone.

I didn't like what I was hearing, but I tapped anyway. I waited a moment, but when Alice didn't come to the door, I put my ear against it. Who could she be talking to in her room? I knew that Ellie and Jack were already in bed, and anyway I could hear only one voice, and that was Alice's. It seemed different, though. It reminded me of something I'd heard before. When I suddenly remembered what it was, I moved my ear away from the wood as if it had been burned and took a big step away from the door.

Her voice was rising and falling, just like Bony Lizzie's had when she'd been standing above the pit, holding a small white thumb bone in each hand.

Almost before I realized what I was doing, I seized

the door handle, turned it, and opened the door wide.

Alice, her mouth opening and closing, was chanting at the mirror. She was sitting on the edge of a straight-backed chair, staring over the top of a candle flame into the dressing-table mirror. I took a deep breath, then crept nearer so as to get a better look.

It was a County spring and after dark, so the room had a chill to it, but despite that there were big beads of sweat on Alice's brow. Even as I watched, two came together and ran down into her left eye and then beyond it onto her cheek like a tear. She was staring into the mirror, her eyes very wide, but when I called her name she never even blinked.

I moved behind the chair and caught the reflection of the brass candlestick in the mirror, but to my horror the face in the mirror above the flame didn't belong to Alice.

It was an old face, haggard and lined, with coarse gray-and-white hair falling like curtains across each gaunt cheek. It was the face of something that had spent a long time in the damp ground.

The eyes moved then, flicking to the left to meet my gaze. They were red points of fire. Although the face cracked into a smile, the eyes were burning with anger and hate.

There was no doubt. It was the face of Mother Malkin.

What was happening? Was Alice already possessed? Or was she somehow using the mirror to talk to Mother Malkin?

Without thinking, I seized the candlestick and swung its heavy base into the mirror, which exploded with a loud crack followed by a glittering, tinkling shower of falling glass. As the mirror shattered, Alice screamed, loud and shrill.

It was the worst screech you can possibly imagine. It was filled with torment, and it reminded me of the noise a pig sometimes makes when it's slaughtered. But I didn't feel sorry for Alice, even though now she was crying and pulling at her hair, her eyes wild and filled with terror.

I was aware that the house was quickly filled with other sounds. The first was the cry of Ellie's baby; the second was a man's deep voice cursing and swearing; the third was big boots stamping down the stairs.

Jack burst furiously into the room. He took one look at the broken mirror, then stepped toward me and raised his fist. I suppose he must have thought it was all my fault, because Alice was still screaming, I was holding the candlestick, and there were small cuts on my knuckles caused by flying glass.

Just in time, Ellie came into the room. She had her baby cradled in her right arm and it was still crying fit to burst, but with her free hand she got a grip on Jack and pulled at him until he unclenched his fist and lowered his arm.

"No, Jack," she pleaded. "What good will that do?"

"I can't believe you've done that," Jack said, glaring at me. "Do you know how old that mirror was? What do you think Dad will say now? How will he feel when he sees this?"

No wonder Jack was angry. It had been bad enough waking everybody up, but that dressing table had belonged to Dad's mam. Now that Dad had given me the tinder-box, it was the last thing he owned that once belonged to his family.

Jack took two steps toward me. The candle hadn't gone out when I'd broken the mirror, but when he shouted again it began to flicker.

"Why did you do it? What on earth's got into you?" he roared.

What could I say? So I just shrugged, then stared down at my boots.

"What are you doing in this room anyway?" Jack persisted.

I didn't answer. Anything I said would only make it worse.

"Stay in your own room from now on!" Jack shouted. "I've a good mind to send the pair of you packing now!"

I glanced toward Alice, who was still sitting on the chair, her head in her hands. She'd stopped crying, but her whole body was shaking.

When I looked back, Jack's anger had given way to alarm. He was staring at Ellie, who suddenly seemed to stagger. Before he could move, she lost her balance and fell back against the wall. Jack forgot about the mirror for a few moments while he fussed over Ellie.

"I don't know what came over me," she said, all flustered. "I suddenly felt light-headed. Oh! Jack! Jack! I nearly dropped the baby!"

"You didn't and she's safe. Don't worry yourself. Here, let me take her. . . ."

Once he had the baby in his arms, Jack calmed down. "For now, just clear this mess up," he told me. "We'll talk about it in the morning."

Ellie walked across to the bed and put her hand on Alice's shoulder. "Alice, you come downstairs for a bit while Tom tidies up," she said. "I'll make us all a drink."

Moments later they'd all gone down to the kitchen, leaving me to pick up the pieces of glass. After about ten minutes I went down there myself to get a brush and pan. They were sitting around the kitchen table sipping herb tea, the baby asleep in Ellie's arms. They weren't talking and nobody offered me a drink. Nobody even glanced in my direction.

I went back upstairs and cleared up the mess as best I could, then went back to my own room. I sat on the bed and stared through the window, feeling terrified and alone. Was Alice already possessed? After all, it had been Mother Malkin's face staring back out of the mirror. If she was, then the baby and everyone else were in real danger.

She hadn't tried to do anything then, but Alice was relatively small compared with Jack, so Mother Malkin would have to be sly. She'd wait for everyone to go to sleep. I'd be the main target. Or maybe the baby. A child's blood would increase her strength.

Or had I broken the mirror just in time? Had I broken the spell at the very moment when Mother Malkin was about to possess Alice? Another possibility was that Alice had just been talking to the witch, using the mirror. Even so, that was bad enough. It meant I had two enemies to worry about.

I needed to do something. But what? While I sat there, my head whirling, trying to think things through, there was a tap on my bedroom door. I thought it was Alice, so

I didn't go. Then a voice called my name softly. It was Ellie, so I opened the door.

"Can we talk inside?" she asked. "I don't want to risk waking the baby. I've only just gotten her off to sleep again."

I nodded, so Ellie came in and carefully closed the door behind her.

"You all right?" she asked, looking concerned.

I nodded miserably but couldn't meet her eyes.

"Would you like to tell me about it?" she asked. "You're a sensible lad, Tom, and you must have had a very good reason for what you did. Talking it through might make you feel better."

How could I tell her the truth? I mean, Ellie had a baby to care for, so how could I tell her that there was a witch somewhere loose in the house with a taste for children's blood? Then I realized that, for the sake of the baby, I would have to tell her something. She had to know just how bad things were. She had to get away.

"There is something, Ellie. But I don't know how to tell you."

Ellie smiled. "The beginning would be as good a place as any . . ."

"Something's followed me back here," I said, looking Ellie straight in the eyes. "Something evil that wants to hurt me. That's why I broke the mirror. Alice was talking to it and—"

Ellie's eyes suddenly flashed with anger. "Tell Jack that, and you certainly *would* feel his fist! You mean you've brought something back here, when I've got a new baby to care for? How could you? How could you do that?"

"I didn't know it was going to happen," I protested. "I only found out tonight. That's why I'm telling you now. You need to leave the house and take the baby to safety. Go now, before it's too late."

"What? Right now? In the middle of the night?"

I nodded.

Ellie shook her head firmly. "Jack wouldn't go. He wouldn't be driven out of his own house in the middle of the night. Not by anything. No, I'll wait. I'm going to stay here, and I'm going to say my prayers. My mother taught me that. She said that if you pray really hard, nothing from the dark can ever harm you. And I really do believe that. Anyway, you could be wrong, Tom," she added. "You're young and only just beginning to learn the job, so it may not be quite as bad as you think. And your mam should be back at any time. If not tonight, then certainly tomorrow night. She'll know what to do. In the meantime, just keep out of that girl's room. There's something not right about her."

As I opened my mouth to speak, intending to have one more go at persuading her to leave, an expression of alarm suddenly came over Ellie's face, and she stumbled and put her hand against the wall to save herself from falling.

"Look what you've done now. I feel faint just thinking about what's going on here."

She sat down on my bed and put her head in her hands while I just stared down at her miserably, not knowing what to do or say.

After a few moments she climbed back to her feet again. "We need to talk to your mam as soon as she gets back, but don't forget, stay away from Alice until then. Do you promise?"

I promised, and with a sad smile Ellie went back to her own room.

It was only when she'd gone that it struck me. . . .

Ellie had stumbled for a second time and said she'd felt light-headed. One stumble could be just chance. Just tiredness. But twice! She was dizzy. Ellie was dizzy, and that was the first sign of possession!

I began to pace up and down. Surely I was wrong. Not Ellie! It couldn't be Ellie. Maybe Ellie was just tired. After all, the baby did keep her awake a lot. But Ellie was strong and healthy. She'd been brought up on a farm herself and wasn't one to let things drag her down. And all that talk about saying prayers. She could have said that so I wouldn't suspect her.

But hadn't Alice told me that Ellie would be difficult to possess? She'd also said that it would probably be Jack, but he hadn't shown any sign of dizziness. Still, there was no denying that he had become more and more bad tempered and aggressive, too! If Ellie hadn't held him back, he'd have thumped my head off my shoulders.

But of course, if Alice were in league with Mother Malkin, *everything* she said would be intended to put me off the scent. I couldn't even trust her account of the Spook's book! She could have told me lies all along! I couldn't read Latin, so there was no way to check what she'd said.

I realized that it could be any one of them. An attack could occur at any moment, and I hadn't any way of knowing who it would come from!

With luck, Mam would be back before dawn. She'd know what to do. But dawn was a long time off, so I couldn't afford to sleep. I'd have to keep watch all night long. If Jack or Ellie were possessed, there was nothing I could do about it. I couldn't go into their room, so all I could do was keep an eye on Alice.

I went outside and sat on the stairs between the door to Ellie and Jack's room and my own. From there I could see Alice's door below. If she left her room, at least I'd be able to give a warning.

I decided that if Mam wasn't back, I'd leave at dawn; apart from her, there was just one more chance of help. . . .

It was a long night, and at first I jumped at the slightest sound—a creak of the stairs or a faint movement of the floorboards in one of the rooms. But gradually I calmed down. It was an old house and these were the noises I was used to—the noises you expected as it slowly settled and cooled down during the night. However, as dawn approached, I started to feel uneasy again.

I began to hear faint scratching noises from inside the walls. It sounded like fingernails clawing at stone, and it wasn't always in the same place. Sometimes it was farther up the stairs on the left; sometimes below, close to Alice's room. It was so faint that it was hard to tell whether I was imagining it or not. But I began to feel cold, really cold, and that told me that danger was near.

Next the dogs began to bark, and within a few minutes the other animals were going crazy, too, the hairy pigs squealing so loud you'd have thought the pig butcher had already arrived. If that wasn't enough, the row started the baby crying again.

I was so cold now that my whole body was shaking and trembling. I just had to do something.

On the riverbank, facing the witch, my hands had known what to do. This time it was my legs that acted faster than I could think. I stood up and ran. Terrified, my heart hammering, I bounded down the stairs, adding to the noise. I just had to get outside and away from the witch. Nothing else mattered. All my courage had gone.

CHAPTER XIII
HAIRY PIGS

I RAN out of the house and headed
north, straight for Hangman's Hill,
still in a panic, only slowing down
when I'd reached the north pasture. I
needed help, and I needed it fast. I
was going back to Chipenden. Only
the Spook could help me now.

Once I'd reached the boundary
fence, the animals suddenly

fell silent, and I turned and looked back toward the farm. Beyond it, I could just see the dirt road winding away in the distance, like a dark stain on the patchwork of gray fields.

It was then that I saw a light on the road. There was a cart moving toward the farm. Was it Mam? For a few moments my hopes were high. But as the cart neared the farm gate, I heard a loud hawking cough, the noise of phlegm being gathered in the throat, and then somebody spat. It was just Snout, the pig butcher. He'd five of our biggest hairy pigs to deal with; once dead, each one took a lot of scraping, so he was making an early start.

He'd never done me any harm, but I was always glad when he'd finished his business and left. Mam had never liked him either. She disliked the way he kept hawking up thick phlegm and spitting it out into the yard.

He was a big man, taller even than Jack, with knotted muscles on his forearms. The muscles were necessary for the work he did. Some pigs weighed more than a man and they fought like mad to avoid the knife. However, there was one part of Snout that had gone to seed. His shirts were always short, with the bottom two buttons open, and his fat, white, hairy belly hung down over the brown leather apron he wore to stop his trousers from getting soaked with blood. He couldn't have been much more than thirty, but his hair was thin and lank.

Disappointed that it wasn't Mam, I watched him unhook the lantern from the cart and begin to unload his tools. He set up for business at the front of the barn, right next to the pigpen.

I'd wasted enough time. I had started to climb over the fence into the wood when, out of the corner of my eye, I saw a movement on the slope below. A shadow was heading my way, hurrying toward the stile at the far end of the north pasture.

It was Alice. I didn't want her following me, but it was better to deal with her now than later, so I sat on the boundary fence and waited for her to reach me. I didn't have to wait long because she ran all the way up the hill.

She didn't come that close but stayed about nine or ten

paces away, her hands on her hips, trying to catch her breath. I looked her up and down, seeing again the black dress and the pointy shoes. I must have woken her up when I'd run down the stairs; to reach me so soon she must have gotten dressed quickly and followed me straightaway.

"I don't want to talk to you," I called across to her, nervousness making my voice wobbly and higher than usual. "Don't waste your time following me either. You've had your chance, so from now on you'd better keep well away from Chipenden."

"You better had talk to me if you know what's good for you," Alice said. "Soon it'll be too late, so there's something you'd better know. Mother Malkin's already here."

"I know that," I said. "I saw her."

"Not just in the mirror, though. It ain't just that. She's back there, somewhere inside the house," Alice said, pointing back down the hill.

"I told you, I know that," I said angrily. "The moonlight showed me the trail she made, and when I came upstairs to tell you that, what did I find? You were already talking to her, and probably not for the first time."

I remembered the first night when I went up to Alice's room and gave her the book. As I went inside, the candle had still been smoking in front of the mirror.

"You probably brought her here," I accused. "You told her where I was."

"Ain't true, that," Alice said, an anger in her voice that matched my own. She took about three steps closer to me. "Sniffed her out, I did, and I used the mirror to see where she was. Didn't realize she was so close, did I? She was too strong for me, so I couldn't break away. Lucky you came in when you did. Lucky for me you broke that mirror."

I wanted to believe Alice, but how could I trust her? When she moved a couple of paces nearer, I half turned, ready to jump down onto the grass on the other side of the fence. "I'm going back to Chipenden to fetch Mr. Gregory," I told her. "He'll know what to do."

"Ain't time for that," said Alice. "When you get back

it'll be too late. There's the baby to think about. Mother Malkin wants to hurt you, but she'll be hungry for human blood. Young blood's what she likes best. That's what makes her strongest."

My fear had made me forget about Ellie's baby. Alice was right. The witch wouldn't want to possess it, but she'd certainly want its blood. When I brought the Spook back, it would be too late.

"But what can I do?" I asked. "What chance have I got against Mother Malkin?"

Alice shrugged and turned down the corners of her mouth. "That's your business. Surely Old Gregory taught you something that could be useful? If you didn't write it down in that notebook of yours, then maybe it's inside your head. You just have to remember it, that's all."

"He's not said that much about witches," I said, suddenly feeling annoyed with the Spook. Most of my training so far had been about boggarts, with little bits on ghasts and ghosts, while all my problems had been caused by witches.

I still didn't trust Alice, but now, after what she'd just said, I couldn't leave for Chipenden. I'd never get the Spook back here in time. Her warning about the threat to Ellie's baby seemed well intentioned, but if Alice were possessed, or on Mother Malkin's side, they were the very words that gave me no choice but to go back down the hill toward the farm. The very words that would keep me from warning the Spook, yet keep me where the witch could get her hands on me at a time of her own choosing.

On the way down the hill, I kept my distance from Alice, but she was at my side when we walked into the yard and crossed close to the front of the barn.

Snout was there, sharpening his knives; he looked up when he saw me and nodded. I nodded back. After he'd nodded at me, he just stared at Alice without speaking, but he looked her up and down twice. Then, just before we reached the kitchen door, he whistled long and loud. Snout's face had more in common with a pig's than with a wolf's, but it was that kind of whistle, heavy with mockery.

Alice pretended not to hear him. Before making the breakfast, she had another job to do: She went straight into the kitchen and started preparing the chicken we'd be having for our midday meal. It was hanging from a hook by the door, its neck off and its insides already pulled out the evening before. She set to work cleaning it with water and salt, her eyes concentrating hard on what she was doing so that her busy fingers wouldn't miss the tiniest bit.

It was then, as I watched her, that I finally remembered something that might just work against a possessed body.

Salt and iron!

I couldn't be sure, but it was worth a try. It was what the Spook used to bind a boggart into a pit, and it might just work against a witch. If I threw it at someone possessed, it might just drive Mother Malkin out.

I didn't trust Alice and didn't want her to see me helping myself to the salt, so I had to wait until she'd stopped cleaning the chicken and left the kitchen. That done, before going out to start my own chores, I paid a visit to Dad's workshop.

It didn't take me long to find what I needed. From among the large collection of files on the shelf above his workbench I chose the biggest and roughest toothed of them all. Soon I was filing away at the edge of an old iron bucket, the noise setting my teeth on edge. But it wasn't long before an even louder noise split the air.

It was the scream of a dying pig, the first of five.

I knew that Mother Malkin could be anywhere, and if she hadn't already possessed someone, she might choose a victim at any moment. So I had to concentrate and be on my guard at all times. But at least now I had something to defend myself with.

Jack wanted me to help Snout, but I was always ready with an excuse, claiming that I was finishing this or just about to do that. If I got stuck working with Snout, I wouldn't be able to keep an eye on everyone else. As I was just his brother visiting for a few days, not the hired help, Jack wasn't able to insist, but he came very close to it.

In the end, after lunch, his face as black as thunder, he was forced to help Snout himself, which was exactly what I wanted. If he was working in front of the barn, I could keep an eye on him from a distance. I kept using excuses to check on Alice and Ellie, too. Either one of them could be possessed, but if it were Ellie, there'd not be much chance of saving the baby: most of the time it was either in her arms or sleeping in its cot close to her side.

I had the salt and iron, but I wasn't sure whether it would be enough. The best thing would have been a silver chain. Even a short one would have been better than nothing. When I was little, I'd once overheard Dad and Mam talking about a silver chain that belonged to her. I'd never seen her wearing one, but it might still be in the house somewhere—maybe in the storeroom just below the attic, which Mam always kept locked.

But their bedroom wasn't locked. Normally I'd never have gone into their room without permission, but I was desperate. I searched Mam's jewelry box. There were brooches and rings in the box, but no silver chain. I searched the whole room. I felt really guilty looking through the drawers, but I did it anyway. I thought there might have been a key to the storeroom, but I didn't find it.

While I was searching, I heard Jack's big boots coming up the stairs. I kept very still, hardly daring to breathe, but he just came up to his bedroom for a few moments and went straight down again. After that, I completed my search but found nothing, so I went down to check on everyone once more.

That day the air had been still and calm, but when I walked by the barn, a breeze had sprung up. The sun was beginning to go down, lighting up everything in a warm, red glow and promising fine weather for the following day. At the front of the barn three dead pigs were now hanging, head down, from big hooks. They were pink and freshly scraped, the last one still dripping blood into a bucket, and Snout was on his knees wrestling with the fourth, which was giving him a hard time of it—it was difficult to tell which of them was grunting the loudest.

Jack, the front of his shirt soaked in blood, glared at me as I passed, but I just smiled and nodded. They were just getting on with the work in hand and there was still quite a bit to do, so they'd be at it long after the sun had set. But so far there wasn't the slightest sign of dizziness, not even a hint of possession.

Within an hour it was dark. Jack and Snout were still working by the light of the fire that was flickering their shadows across the yard.

The horror began as I went to the shed at the back of the barn to fetch a bag of spuds from the storeroom.

I heard a scream. It was a scream filled with terror. The scream of a woman facing the very worst thing that could possibly happen to her.

I dropped the sack of potatoes and ran around to the front of the barn. There I came to a sudden halt, hardly able to believe what I was seeing.

Ellie was standing about twenty paces away, holding out both her arms, screaming and screaming as if she were being tortured. At her feet lay Jack, blood all over his face. I thought Ellie was screaming because of Jack—but no, it was because of Snout.

He was facing toward me, as if he were waiting for me to arrive. In his left hand he was holding his favorite sharp knife, the long one he always used to cut a pig's throat. I froze in horror, because I knew what I'd heard in Ellie's scream.

With his right arm, he was cradling her baby.

There was thick pig blood on Snout's boots, and it was still dripping onto them from his apron. He moved the knife closer to the baby.

"Come here, boy," he called in my direction. "Come to me." Then he laughed.

His mouth had opened and closed as he spoke, but it wasn't his voice that came out. It was Mother Malkin's. Neither was it his usual deep belly rumble of laughter. It was the cackle of the witch.

I took a slow step toward Snout. Then another one. I wanted to get closer to him. I wanted to save Ellie's baby. I tried to go faster. But I couldn't. My feet felt as heavy as lead. It was like desperately trying to run in a nightmare. My legs were moving as if they didn't belong to me.

I suddenly realized something that brought me out in a cold sweat. I wasn't just moving toward Snout because I wanted to. It was because Mother Malkin had summoned me. She was drawing me toward him at the pace she wanted, drawing me toward his waiting knife. I wasn't going to the rescue. I was just going to die. I was under some sort of spell. A spell of compulsion.

I'd felt something similar down by the river, but just in time my left hand and arm had acted by themselves to knock Mother Malkin into the water. Now my limbs were as powerless as my mind.

I was moving closer to Snout. Closer and closer to his waiting knife. His eyes were the eyes of Mother Malkin, and his face was bulging horribly. It was as if the witch inside were distorting its shape, swelling the cheeks close to bursting, bulging the eyes close to popping, beetling the brow into craggy overhanging cliffs; below them the bulbous, protruding eyes were centered with fire, casting a red, baleful glow before them.

I took another step and felt my heart thud. Another

step and it thudded again. I was much nearer to Snout by now. *Thud, thud* went my heart, a beat for each step.

When I was no more than five paces from the waiting knife, I heard Alice running toward us, screaming my name. I saw her out of the corner of my eye, moving out of the darkness into the glow from the fire. She was heading straight toward Snout, her black hair streaming back from her head as if she were running directly into a gale.

Without even breaking her stride, she kicked toward Snout with all her might. She aimed just above his leather apron, and I watched the toe of her pointy shoe disappear so deeply into his fat belly that only the heel was visible.

Snout gasped, doubled over, and dropped Ellie's baby, but, lithe like a year-old cat, Alice dropped to her knees and caught it just before it hit the ground. Then she spun away, running back toward Ellie.

At the very moment that Alice's pointy shoe touched Snout's belly, the spell was broken. I was free again. Free to move my own limbs. Free to move. Or free to attack.

Snout was almost bent in two, but he straightened back up, and although he'd dropped the baby, he was still holding the knife. I watched as he moved it toward me. He staggered a bit, too—perhaps he was dizzy, or maybe it was just a reaction to Alice's pointy shoe.

Free of the spell, a whole range of feelings surged up inside me. There was sorrow for what had been done to Jack, horror at the danger Ellie's baby had been in, and anger that this could happen to my family. And in that moment I knew that I was born to be a spook. The very best spook who'd ever lived. I could and would make Mam proud of me.

You see, rather than being filled with fear, I was all ice and fire. Deep inside I was raging, full of hot anger that was threatening to explode. While on the outside I was as cold as ice, my mind sharp and clear, my breathing slow.

I thrust my hands into my breeches pockets. Then I brought them out fast, each fist full of what it had found there, and hurled each handful straight at Snout's head, something white from my right hand and something dark from my left. They came together, a white and a black cloud, just as they struck his face and shoulders.

Salt and iron — the same mixture so effective against a boggart. Iron to bleed away its strength; salt to burn it. Iron filings from the edge of the old bucket and salt from Mam's kitchen store. I was just hoping that it would have the same effect on a witch.

I suppose having a mixture like that thrown into your face wouldn't do anybody much good — at the very least it would make you cough and splutter — but the effect on Snout was much worse than that. First he opened his hand and let the knife fall. Then his eyes rolled up into his head and he pitched slowly forward, down onto his knees. Then he hit his forehead very hard on the ground, and his face twisted to one side.

Something thick and slimy began to ooze out of his left nostril. I just stood there watching, unable to move as Mother Malkin slowly bubbled and twisted from his nose into the shape that I remembered. It was her all right, but some of her was the same, while other bits were different.

For one thing, she was less than a third of the size she'd been the last time I saw her. Now her shoulders were hardly past my knees, but she was still wearing the long cloak, which was trailing on the ground, and the gray-and-white hair still fell onto her hunched shoulders like mildewy curtains. It was her skin that was really different. All glistening, strange, and sort of twisted and stretched. However, the red eyes hadn't changed, and they glared at me once before she turned and began to move away toward the corner of the barn. She seemed to be shrinking even more, and I wondered if that was the salt and iron still having an effect. I didn't know what more I could do, so I just stood there watching her go, too exhausted to move.

Alice wasn't having that. By now she'd handed the baby to Ellie, and she came running across and made straight for the fire. She picked up a piece of wood that was burning at one end, then ran at Mother Malkin, holding it out in front of her.

I knew what she was going to do. One touch, and the witch would go up in flames. Something inside me couldn't let that happen because it was too horrible, so I caught Alice by the arm as she ran past and spun her around so that she dropped the burning log.

She turned on me, her face full of fury, and I thought I was about to feel a pointy shoe. Instead she gripped my forearm so tightly that her fingernails actually bit deep into the flesh.

"Get harder or you won't survive!" she hissed into my face. "Just doing what Old Gregory says won't be enough. You'll die like the others!"

She released my arm, and I looked down at it and saw beads of blood where her nails had cut into me.

"You have to burn a witch," Alice said, the anger in her voice lessening, "to make sure they don't come back. Putting them in the ground ain't no good. It just delays things. Old Gregory knows that, but he's too soft to use burning. Now it's too late. . . ."

Mother Malkin was disappearing around the side of

the barn into the shadows, still shrinking with each step, her black cloak trailing on the ground behind her.

It was then that I realized the witch had made a big mistake. She'd taken the wrong route, right across the largest pigpen. By now she was small enough to fit under the lowest plank of wood.

The pigs had had a very bad day. Five of their number had been slaughtered, and it had been a very noisy, messy business that had probably scared them pretty badly. So they weren't best pleased, to say the least, and it probably wasn't a good time to go into their pen. And big hairy pigs will eat anything, anything at all. Soon it was Mother Malkin's turn to scream, and it went on for a long time.

"Could be as good as burning, that," said Alice when the sound finally faded away. I could see the relief in her face. I felt the same. We were both glad it was all over. I was tired, so I just shrugged, not sure what to think, but I was already looking back toward Ellie, and I didn't like what I saw.

Ellie was frightened, and she was horrified. She was looking at us as if she couldn't believe what had happened and what we'd done. It was as if she'd seen me properly for the first time. As if she'd suddenly realized what I was.

I understood something, too. For the first time I really felt what it was like to be the Spook's apprentice. I'd seen people move to the other side of the road to avoid passing close to us. I'd watched them shiver or cross themselves just because we'd passed through their village, but I hadn't taken it personally. In my mind it was their reaction to the Spook, not to me.

But I couldn't ignore this, or push it to the side of my mind. It was happening to me directly, and it was happening in my own home.

I suddenly felt more alone than I ever had before.

CHAPTER XIV
THE SPOOK'S ADVICE

B_{UT} not everything turned out badly. Jack wasn't dead after all. I didn't like to ask too many questions because it just got everybody upset, but it seemed that one minute Snout had been about to start scraping the belly of the fifth pig with Jack, and the next he'd suddenly gone berserk and attacked him.

It was just pig's blood on Jack's face. He'd been knocked unconscious with a piece of timber. Snout had then gone into the house and snatched the baby. He'd wanted to use it as bait to get me close so that he could use his knife on me.

Of course, the way I'm telling it now isn't quite right. It wasn't really Snout doing these terrible things. He'd been possessed, and Mother Malkin was just using his body. After a couple of hours Snout recovered and went home puzzled and nursing a very sore belly. He didn't seem to remember anything about what had happened, and none of us wanted to enlighten him.

Nobody slept much that night. After building the fire up high, Ellie stayed down in the kitchen all night and wouldn't let the baby out of her sight. Jack went to bed nursing a sore head, but he kept waking up and having to dash outside to be sick in the yard.

An hour or so before dawn, Mam came home. She didn't seem very happy either. It was as if something had gone wrong.

I lifted her bag to carry it into the house. "Are you all right, Mam?" I asked. "You look tired."

"Never mind me, son. What's happened here? I can tell something's wrong just by looking at your face."

"It's a long story," I said. "We'd better get inside first."

When we walked into the kitchen Ellie was so relieved to see Mam that she started to cry, and that set the baby off crying, too. Jack came down then and everybody tried to tell Mam things at once, but I gave up after a few seconds because Jack started off on one of his rants.

Mam shut him up pretty quickly. "Lower your voice, Jack," she told him. "This is still my house, and I can't abide shouting."

He wasn't happy at being told off in front of Ellie like that, but he knew better than to argue.

She made each one of us tell her exactly what had happened, starting with Jack. I was the last, and when it was my turn, she sent Ellie and Jack up to bed so that we could talk alone. Not that she said much. She just listened quietly, then held my hand.

Finally she went up to Alice's room and spent a long time talking to her alone.

The sun had been up less than an hour when the Spook arrived. Somehow I'd been expecting him. He waited at the gate, and I went out and told the tale again, while he leaned on his staff. When I'd finished, he shook his head.

"I sensed that something was wrong, lad, but I came too late. Still you did all right. You used your initiative and managed to remember some of the things I'd taught you. If all else fails, you can always fall back on salt and iron."

"Should I have let Alice burn Mother Malkin?" I asked.

He sighed and scratched at his beard. "As I told you, it's a cruel thing to burn a witch, and I don't hold with it myself."

"I suppose now I'll have to face Mother Malkin again," I said.

The Spook smiled. "No, lad, you can rest easy, because

she won't be coming back to this world. Not after what happened at the end. Remember what I told you about eating the heart of a witch? Well, those pigs of yours did it for us."

"Not just the heart. They ate up every bit," I told him. "So I'm safe? Really safe? She can't come back?"

"Aye, you're safe from Mother Malkin. There are other threats out there just as bad, but you're safe for now."

I felt a big sense of relief, as if a heavy weight had been lifted from my shoulders. I'd been living in a nightmare, and now, with the threat of Mother Malkin removed, the world seemed a much brighter, happier place. It was over at last, and I could start to look forward to things again.

"Well, you're safe until you make another silly mistake," the Spook added. "And don't say you won't. He who never makes a mistake never makes anything. It's part of learning the job.

"Well, what's to be done now?" he asked, squinting into the rising sun.

"About what?" I asked, wondering what he meant.

"About the girl, lad," he said. "It looks like it's the pit for her. I don't see any way around it."

"But she saved Ellie's baby at the end," I protested. "She saved my life as well."

"She used the mirror, lad. It's a bad sign. Lizzie taught her a lot. Too much. Now she's shown us that she's prepared to use it. What will she do next?"

"But she meant well. She used it to try and find Mother Malkin."

"Maybe, but she knows too much, and she's clever, too. She's just a girl now, but one day she'll be a woman, and some clever women are dangerous."

"My mam's clever," I told him, annoyed at what he'd said. "But she's good, too. Everything she does she does for the best. She uses her brains to help people. One year, when I was really small, the ghasts on Hangman's Hill frightened me so much that I couldn't sleep. Mam went up there after dark and she shut them up. They were quiet for months and months."

I could have added that, on our first morning together,

the Spook had told me that there wasn't much to be done about ghasts. And that Mam had proved him wrong. But I didn't. I'd blurted out too much already, and it didn't need to be said.

The Spook didn't say anything. He was staring toward the house.

"Ask my mam what she thinks about Alice," I suggested. "She seems to get on well with her."

"I was going to do that anyway," said the Spook. "It's about time we had a little talk. You wait here until we're finished."

I watched the Spook cross the yard. Even before he reached it, the kitchen door opened and Mam welcomed him over the threshold.

Later, it was possible to work out some of the things that they'd said to each other, but they talked together for almost half an hour, and I never did find out whether ghasts came into the conversation. When the Spook finally came out into the sunshine, Mam stayed in the doorway. He did something unusual then — something I'd never seen him do before. At first I thought he'd just nodded at Mam as he said good-bye, but there was a bit more to it than that. There was a movement of his shoulders, too. It was slight but very definite, so there was no doubt about it. As he took his leave of Mam, the Spook gave her a little bow.

When he crossed the yard toward me, he seemed to be smiling to himself. "I'll be off on my way back to Chipenden now," he said, "but I think your mother would like you to stay one more night. Anyway, I'm going to leave it up to you," said the Spook. "Either bring the girl back and we'll bind her in the pit, or take her to her aunt in Staumin. The choice is yours. Use your instinct for what's right. You'll know what to do."

Then he was gone, leaving me with my head whirling. I knew what I wanted to do about Alice, but it had to be the right thing.

○ ○ ○

So I got to eat another of Mam's suppers.

Dad was back by then, but although Mam was happy to see him, there was something not quite right, a sort of atmosphere like an invisible cloud hanging over the table. So it wasn't exactly a celebration party, and nobody had much to say.

The food was good, though, one of Mam's special hot pots, so I didn't mind the lack of conversation — I was too busy filling my belly and getting second helpings before Jack could scrape the dish clean.

Jack had his appetite back, but he was a bit subdued, like everyone else. He'd been through a lot, with a big bump on his forehead to prove it. As for Alice, I hadn't told her what the Spook had said, but I felt she knew anyway. She didn't speak once during dinner. But the quietest one of all was Ellie. Despite the joy of having her baby back, what she'd seen had upset her badly, and I could tell it would take some getting over.

When the others went up to bed, Mam asked me to stay behind. I sat by the fire in the kitchen, just as I had on the night before I went away to begin my apprenticeship. But something in her face told me this conversation was going to be different. Before, she'd been firm with me but hopeful. Confident that things would work out all right. Now she looked sad and uncertain.

"I've been delivering County babies for nearly twenty-five years," she said, sitting down in her rocking chair, "and I've lost a few. Although it's very sad for the mother and father, it's just something that happens. It happens with farm animals, Tom. You've seen it yourself."

I nodded. Every year a few lambs were born dead. It was something you expected.

"This time it was worse," Mam said. "This time both the mother and the baby died, something that's never happened to me before. I know the right herbs and how to blend them. I know how to cope with severe bleeding. I know just what to do. And this mother was young and strong. She shouldn't have died, but I couldn't save her. I did everything I could, but I couldn't save her. And it's given me a pain here. A pain in my heart."

Mam gave a sort of sob and clutched at her chest. For one awful moment I thought she was going to cry, but then she took a deep breath and the strength came back into her face.

"But sheep die, Mam, and sometimes cows when giving birth," I told her. "A mother was bound to die eventually. It's a miracle that you've gone so long without it happening before."

I did my best, but it was hard to console her. Mam was taking it very badly. It made her look on the gloomy side of things.

"It's getting darker, son," she said to me. "And it's coming sooner than I expected. I'd hoped you'd be a grown man first, with years of experience under your belt. So you're going to have to listen carefully to everything your master says. Every little thing will count. You're going to have to get yourself ready as quickly as you can and work hard at your Latin lessons."

She paused then and held out her hand. "Let me see the book."

When I handed it to her, she flicked through the pages, pausing every so often to read a few lines. "Did it help?" she asked.

"Not much," I admitted.

"Your master wrote this himself. Did he tell you that?"

I shook my head. "Alice said it was written by a priest."

Mam smiled. "Your master was a priest once. That's how he started out. No doubt he'll tell you about it one day. But don't ask. Let him tell you in his own good time."

"Was that what you and Mr. Gregory talked about?" I asked.

"That and other things, but mainly about Alice. He asked me what I thought should happen to her. I told him he should leave it to you. So have you made up your mind yet?"

I shrugged. "I'm still not sure what to do, but Mr. Gregory said that I should use my instincts."

"That's good advice, son," Mam said.

"But what do you think, Mam?" I asked. "What did you tell Mr. Gregory about Alice? Is Alice a witch? Tell me that at least."

"No," Mam said slowly, weighing her words carefully. "She's not a witch, but she will be one day. She was born with the heart of a witch, and she's little choice but to follow that path."

"Then she should go into the pit at Chipenden," I said sadly, hanging my head.

"Remember your lessons," Mam said sternly. "Remember what your master taught you. There's more than one kind of witch."

"The benign," I said. "You mean Alice might turn out to be a good witch who helps others?"

"She might. And she might not. Do you know what I really think? You might not want to hear this."

"I do," I said.

"Alice might end up neither good nor bad. She might end up somewhere in between. That would make her very dangerous to know. That girl could be the bane of your life, a blight, a poison on everything you do. Or she might turn out to be the best and strongest friend you'll ever have. Someone who'll make all the difference in the world. I just don't know which way it will go. I can't see it, no matter how hard I try."

"How could you see it anyway, Mam?" I asked. "Mr. Gregory said he doesn't believe in prophecy. He said the future's not fixed."

Mam put a hand on my shoulder and gave me a little squeeze of reassurance. "There's some choice open to us all," she said. "But maybe one of the most important decisions you'll ever make will be about Alice. Go to bed now, and get a good night's sleep if you can. Make up your mind tomorrow when the sun's shining."

One thing I didn't ask Mam was how she'd managed to silence the ghasts on Hangman's Hill. It was my instincts again. I just knew that it was something she wouldn't want to talk about. In a family, there are some things you don't ask. You know you'll be told when it's the right time.

❂ ❂ ❂

We left soon after dawn, my heart down in my boots.

Ellie followed me to the gate. I stopped there but waved Alice on, and she sauntered up the hill, swinging her hips, without even once glancing back.

"I need to say something to you, Tom," Ellie said. "It hurts me to do it, but it has to be said."

I could tell by her voice that it was going to be bad. I nodded miserably and forced myself to meet her eyes. I was shocked to see that they were streaming with tears.

"You're still welcome here, Tom," Ellie said, brushing her hair back from her forehead and trying to smile. "That's not changed. But we do have to think of our child. So you'll be welcome here, but not after dark. You see, that's what's made Jack so bad tempered recently. I didn't like to tell you just how strongly he feels, but it has to be said now. He doesn't like the job you're doing at all. Not one little bit. It gives him the creeps. And he's scared for the baby.

"We're frightened, you see. We're frightened that if

you're ever here after dark, you might attract something else. You might bring back something bad with you, and we can't risk anything happening to our family. Come and visit us during the day, Tom. Come and see us when the sun's up and the birds are singing."

Ellie hugged me then, and that made it even worse. I knew that something had come between us and that things had changed forever. I felt like crying, but somehow I stopped myself. I don't know how I managed it. There was a big lump in my throat, and I couldn't speak.

I watched Ellie walk back to the farmhouse and turned my attention back to the decision I had to make.

What should I do about Alice?

I'd woken up certain that it was my duty to take her back with me to Chipenden. It seemed the right thing to do. The safe thing to do. It felt like a duty. When I gave Mother Malkin the cakes, I'd let the softness of my heart overrule me. And look where that had gotten me. So it was probably best to deal with Alice now, before it was too late. As the Spook said, you had to think of the innocents who might be harmed in the future.

On the first day of the journey, we didn't speak to each other much. I just told her we were going back to Chipenden to see the Spook. If Alice knew what was going to happen to her, she certainly didn't complain. Then on the second day, as we got closer to the village and were actually on the lower slopes of the fells, no more than a mile or so from the Spook's house, I told Alice what I'd been keeping bottled up inside me; what had been worrying me ever since I'd realized just what the cakes contained.

We were sitting on a grassy bank close to the side of the road. The sun had set and the light was beginning to fail.

"Alice, do you ever tell lies?" I asked.

"Everybody tells lies sometimes," she replied. "Wouldn't be human if you didn't. But mostly I tell the truth."

"What about that night when I was trapped in the pit? When I asked you about those cakes. You said there hadn't been another child at Lizzie's house. Was that true?"

"Didn't see one."

"The first one that went missing was no more than a baby. It couldn't have wandered off by itself. Are you sure?"

Alice nodded and then bowed her head, staring down at the grass.

"I suppose it could have been carried off by wolves," I said. "That's what the village lads thought."

"Lizzie said she's seen wolves in these parts. That could be it," Alice agreed.

"So what about the cakes, Alice? What was in them?"

"Suet and pork bits mostly. Bread crumbs, too."

"What about the blood, then? Animal blood wouldn't have been good enough for Mother Malkin. Not when she needed enough strength to bend the bars over the pit. So where did the blood come from, Alice—the blood that was used in the cakes?"

Alice started to cry. I waited patiently for her to finish, then asked the question again.

"Well, where did it come from?"

"Lizzie said I was still a child," Alice said. "They'd used my blood lots of times. So one more time didn't matter. It don't hurt that much. Not when you get used to it. How could I stop Lizzie anyway?"

With that, Alice pushed up her sleeve and showed me her upper arm. There was still enough light to see the scars. And there were a lot of them—some old; some relatively new. The newest one of all hadn't healed properly yet. It was still weeping.

"There's more than that. Lots more. But I can't show 'em all," Alice said.

I didn't know what to say, so I just kept quiet. But I'd already made up my mind, and soon we walked off into the dark, away from Chipenden.

I'd decided to take Alice straight to Staumin, where her aunt lived. I couldn't bear the thought of her ending up in a pit in the Spook's garden. It was just too terrible—and I remembered another pit. I remembered how Alice had helped me from Tusk's pit just before Bony Lizzie had come to collect my bones. But above all, it was what Alice had just told me that had finally changed my mind. Once, she'd been one of the innocents. Alice had been a victim, too.

We climbed Parlick Pike, then moved north onto Blindhurst Fell, always keeping to the high ground.

I liked the idea of going to Staumin. It was near the coast, and I'd never seen the sea before, except from the tops of the fells. The route I chose was more than a bit out of the way, but I fancied exploring and liked being up there close to the sun. Anyway, Alice didn't seem to mind at all.

It was a good journey, and I enjoyed Alice's company, and for the first time we really started to talk. She taught me a lot, too. She knew the names of more stars than I did and was really good at catching rabbits.

As for plants, Alice was an expert on things that the Spook hadn't even mentioned so far, such as deadly nightshade and mandrake. I didn't believe everything she said, but I wrote it down anyway because she'd been taught it by Lizzie and I thought it was useful to learn what a witch believes. Alice was really good at distinguishing mushrooms from poisonous toadstools, some of which were so dangerous that one bite would stop your heart or drive you insane. I had my notebook with me and under the heading called *Botany*, I added three more pages of useful information.

One night, when we were less than a day's walk from Staumin, we stayed in a forest clearing. We'd just cooked two rabbits in the embers of a fire until the meat almost melted in our mouths. After the meal Alice did something really strange. After turning to face me, she reached across and held my hand.

We sat there like that for a long time. She was staring into the embers of the fire, and I was looking up at the stars. I didn't want to break away, but I was all mixed up. My left hand was holding her left hand and I felt guilty. I felt as if I were holding hands with the dark, and I knew the Spook wouldn't like it.

There was no way I could get away from the truth. Alice was going to be a witch one day. It was then that I realized Mam was right. It was nothing to do with prophecy. You could see it in Alice's eyes. She'd always be somewhere in between, neither wholly good nor wholly bad. But wasn't that true of all of us? Not one of us was perfect.

So I didn't pull my hand away. I just sat there, one part of me enjoying holding her hand, which was sort of comforting after all that had happened, while the other part sweated with guilt.

It was Alice who broke away. She took her hand out of mine and then touched my arm where her nails had cut me on the night we destroyed Mother Malkin. You could see the scars clearly in the glow from the embers.

"Put my brand on you there," she said with a smile. "That won't ever fade away."

I thought that was a strange thing to say, and I wasn't sure what she meant. Back home we put our brand on cattle. We did it to show that they belonged to us and to stop strays getting mixed up with animals from neighboring farms. So how could I belong to Alice?

The following day we came down onto a great flat plain. Some of it was moss land and the worst bits were soggy marsh, but eventually we found our way through to Staumin. I never got to see the aunt because she wouldn't come out to talk to me. Still, she agreed to take Alice in, so I couldn't complain.

There was a big, wide river nearby, and before I left for Chipenden, we walked down its bank as far as the sea. I wasn't really taken with it. It was a gray, windy day, and the water was the same color as the sky and the waves were big and rough.

"You'll be all right here," I said, trying to be cheerful. "It'll be nice when the sun shines."

"Just have to make the best of it," Alice said. "Can't be worse than Pendle."

I suddenly felt sorry for her again. I felt lonely at times, but at least I had the Spook to talk to; Alice didn't even know her aunt properly, and the rough sea made everything seem bleak and cold.

"Look, Alice, I don't expect we'll see each other again, but if you ever need help, try to get word to me," I offered.

I suppose I said that because Alice was the nearest thing to a friend I had. And as a promise, it wasn't quite as daft as the first one I'd made her. I didn't commit myself to actually doing anything. Next time she asked for any-thing, I'd be talking to the Spook first.

To my surprise, Alice smiled, and she had a strange look in her eyes. It reminded me of what Dad had once said about women sometimes knowing things that men don't—and when you suspect that, you should never ask what they're thinking.

"Oh, we'll meet again," Alice said. "Ain't no doubt about that."

"I'll have to be off now," I said, turning to leave.

"I'll miss you, Tom," Alice said. "Won't be the same without you."

"I'll miss you, too, Alice," I said, giving her a smile.

As the words came out, I thought that I'd said them out of politeness. But I hadn't been on the road more than ten minutes before I knew I was wrong.

I'd meant every word, and I was feeling lonely already.

I'VE written most of this from memory, but some of it from my notebook and my diary. I'm back at Chipenden now, and the Spook is pleased with me. He thinks I'm making really good progress.

Bony Lizzie's in the pit where the Spook used to keep Mother Malkin. The bars have been straightened out, and she certainly won't be getting any midnight cakes from me. As for Tusk, he's buried in the hole he dug for my grave.

Poor Billy Bradley's back in his grave outside the churchyard at Layton, but at least he's got his thumbs now. None of it's pleasant, but it's something that just goes with the job. You have to like it or lump it, as my dad says.

There's something else I should tell you. The Spook agrees with what Mam said. He thinks that the winters are getting longer and that the dark is growing in power. He's sure that the job's getting harder and harder.

So keeping that in mind, I'll carry on studying and learning—as my mam once told me, you never know just what you can do until you try. So I'm going to try. I'm going to try just as hard as I possibly can because I want her to be really proud of me.

Now I'm just an apprentice, but one day I'll be the Spook.

THOMAS J. WARD

The Journal of
THOMAS J. WARD

Boggarts

Hairy Boggarts

Can be friendly or hostile or a mixture of both.
Have coarse hairy coats and take on different
animal shapes—mainly dogs but lots of cats and a
few goats. Can also be shaped like horses. Lots of hairy
boggarts in the County! There's a horse boggart at
Hackensall. Black dog boggarts to be found at Warton
and up on the Long Ridge.

Hall Knockers

Boggarts that rap on walls or doors and cause a nuisance.
Often get up to tricks. May throw pots and pans around in
kitchen, smash cups and saucers, and wake up household.
Pull bedclothes from bed. Dangerous because unpredictable.
Can change without notice into stone chuckers. These are
boggarts that throw pebbles or even boulders. All types of
boggart are ranked from one to ten. One is the most powerful.
Can kill. Sometimes, stone chuckers make showers of
stones rain down on a village or house for weeks at a time.
Need to be artificially bound.

Cattle Rippers

Cattle rippers are boggarts that drink blood from cattle.
Can cause farmer hardship. Sometimes change without warning
into full-blown rippers, which are boggarts that drink blood
from humans. These always kill but sometimes very slowly.

WITCHES

four Types of Witches

The <u>malevolent</u>, which means evil. Spook said no local witch problem now. East, near Pendle Hill, there are lots of malevolent witches.

The <u>benign</u>, which means good. Good witches help neighbors and wider community. Sometimes people travel far and wide to see them. Usually charge a fee. Sometimes work for nothing. Cure warts, coughs, fevers, and other ailments. Experts on herbs. Call themselves "healers" rather than witches. Church treats them no differently than the malevolent. Thinks them in league with the Devil. If caught both types of witches are burned.

The <u>falsely accused</u> are blamed for witchcraft in error. Sometimes tortured. Often their homes are seized and sold. If witchfinder involved, property usually confiscated. He makes a living this way. Allegations sometimes made by jealous neighbors who share proceeds with witchfinder.

The <u>unaware</u> means a witch who doesn't know she's a witch. Sometimes able to hurt others by harboring resentments. Evil wishing. Evil eye. Unaware can either be malevolent or benign. The latter always have a good effect on those around them. Being unaware can sometimes last a lifetime.

More on Witches

Some use bone magic. Victim nearly always dies of shock or blood loss. Finger and thumb and rib bones are the most useful. Seventh rib most of all. Bones usually taken just before dawn.

Malevolent witches usually bone bound after death. Spirits trapped in their bones. To stop them scratching their way to the surface, thirteen iron bars should be used, set into stone. Also helps to bury them head downward. Close to roots of a tree if possible.

A very powerful malevolent witch can be undead ... Can crawl, slither, or drag her way toward her victim. Body will be soft and pliable and able to ooze into a victim's ears or nose and possess his body. Making sure she doesn't come back is difficult. Can burn or eat the witch's heart, but both ways too barbaric. Pit is the only method the Spook approves of.

Swimming

One of the main tests for a witch. Suspected witch has feet tied to hands. Thrown into nearest pond or lake. Sinking means innocent. Floating means guilty. If old, usually die of shock anyway. Especially in winter. Mam says it's a test carried out by fools.

Village Girls with Pointy Shoes

Warned about the village girls. Get up to all sorts of tricks. Especially need to take care with any who wear pointy shoes. They're not to be trusted.

Met Alice, a girl who actually wears pointy shoes! She was nice to me but terrified some of the village lads.

Must be on my guard.

THE UNQUIET DEAD

USUALLY FALL INTO TWO CATEGORIES

Ghasts are fragments of spirits that have moved on. Leaving bad part of themselves behind makes them able to do this. Ghasts are repetitive, doing the same thing over and over again. Usually something done at scene of crime. Something violent like a murder. Ghasts can only harm you if you're afraid. Also ranked from one to ten. Most people hardly aware of a ten. Ghasts of the highest rank can drive people insane through fear. Sometimes they try to touch you. Squeeze your throat or press on chest to make it hard to breathe.

Ghosts are full spirits still trapped on earth and unable to pass on. Sometimes because of some crime they have committed. Others have a message for people still alive. May linger years until their task is completed. Sometimes ghosts don't know they're dead. Can sometimes be given a talking-to and asked to move on. These are also ranked from one to ten. Ones can be really dangerous and can choose whether to make themselves visible or not. Most are malevolent.

How to Bind a Boggart

Boggarts move up and down ley lines but can be trapped in one place. This is called naturally bound. Some think the lines are ancient paths used by forefathers in ancient times. But they're really lines of power underground. Invisible roads that some boggarts use to travel quickly from place to place. Earthquakes can trap boggarts and make them naturally bound, unable to move more than a dozen paces in any direction. Most best left where they are. If in awkward spot (near house or road), need to be moved away and artificially bound as follows:

- Pit needs to be dug at least six feet deep.
  For rippers, nine feet.
- Pit must be coated with mixture of salt
  and iron mixed into a bone glue.
- Salt burns a boggart.
  Iron bleeds away its strength.
- Blood placed in pit to lure boggart into it before
  stone is dropped into place, sealing it underground.
- Don't forget to coat inside of stone!

Need to employ help of tradesmen. Mason. Rigger. List of County tradesmen with this experience in Spook's library.

NEED TO MEMORIZE THEM
ALL BEFORE END OF FIRST YEAR!

Information on Mother Malkin from the Spook's Book on Witches

Mother Malkin uses blood magic. Gets her power from human blood—mainly that of children! Once lived on farm to west of the County. Gave home and support to young women (without husbands) who were expecting babies. Blood of babies used for magic. Some of women never seen again. Has a son called Tusk. Very strong and dangerous.

Later, locals dug up bodies of women. Many had been crushed. Ribs broken. Tusk did it. Wherever Mother Malkin lived there'd been trouble. Last stay was near Chipenden. Spook drove Lizzie away and put Malkin in pit.

Possession:
The Damned, the Dizzy, and the Desperate

Spook lent me book from his library (title above) all about possession. Said it was the "definitive work." Best book ever written on the subject. Not much help at the moment. It's in Latin, a language I'm going to start learning soon. I don't know what the title means but I'm scared. Couldn't be more desperate myself.

What Alice told me about Possession

Alice explained title of the Spook's book, <u>The Damned,</u> <u>the Dizzy, and the Desperate</u>. First word just used by priests for those they think certain to go to Hell. Second word much more useful. A body newly possessed has poor balance and keeps falling over. So that's how you can tell they're newly possessed. The possessed may be bad tempered, too. So sudden change of personality may give warning. Calm and placid person may become irritable.

"Desperate" is the state of an undead witch wanting to possess new healthy body. Once that's achieved, she's desperate to keep it. So very dangerous. Capable of anything.

Men easier to possess than women. Very dangerous if Mother Malkin possesses someone big and strong like Jack.

Original soul is still trapped in body. Can't just kill body to get rid of possessor. That's as bad as murder! So book not clear on what can be done. Seems unfinished.

What Alice told me about Botany

Plants have lots of uses.

They can kill, cure, or drive you insane!

Deadly nightshade is also called belladonna, which means "beautiful lady." Can be used as ointment to make a woman's eyes bright and attractive. Very risky and dangerous, but is sometimes eaten by witches. Eat too much and you die or are driven mad! A small amount can be used to see into the future. Pendle witches use it to fly! Alice said they make an ointment from it and smear it on their bodies. But she'd never seen a witch actually fly.

Mandrake. Also called mandragora. Can be recognized by pale blue flowers and large leaves. Some witches call its berries "Devil's Apples." Eating the plant can make you fall unconscious. Too much and you never wake up. Or wake up insane. Can be used as purge to cleanse poisons from body. Helps relieve toothache and pains in the joints. Also used as ingredient in love potions. Roots are shaped like a human body. Supposed to shriek when pulled from the ground. Alice hasn't heard that but Bony Lizzie said it's true. Mandrakes are best looked for at crossroads but are rare in the County.

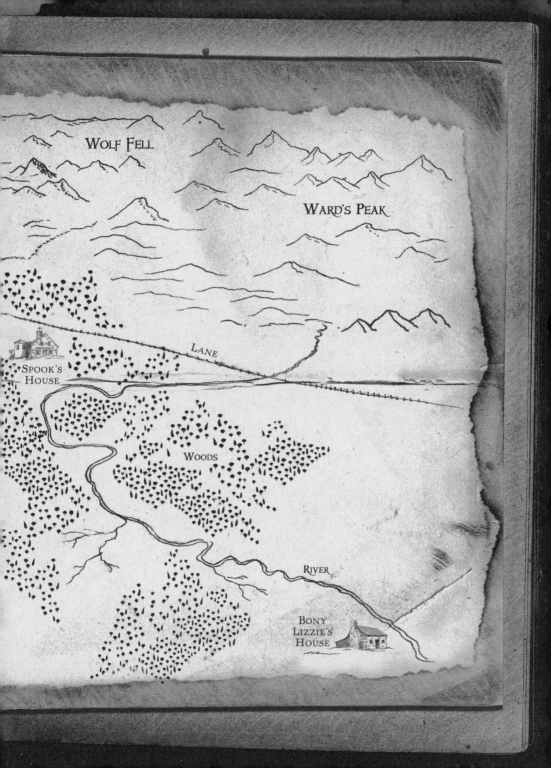

Symbols

BOGGARTS

Beta for Boggart

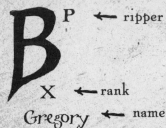

P ← ripper

X ← rank

Gregory ← name

I — dangerous
X — hardly detectable

Naturally bound boggart

Artificially bound boggart

GHOSTS/GHASTS

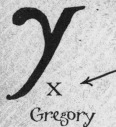

X

Gregory

I — dangerous
X — hardly detectable

WITCHES

M

Gregory

M   malevolent
B   benign
U   unaware